To Kimie, my forever muse; thank you for always being my Sarah, even long before we ever met. xo

Panic. Amidst the sea of emotions with which her fractured sleep had besieged her, that was the one most prevalent now. Sheer and absolute panic.

Samantha Collins slammed her hand down in the dark, frantically fumbling around for the the snooze button to her alarm clock. Eyes still closed, she lifted her head and stretched, her fingers at last hitting upon the elusive bar, and finally halting the early morning radio music with a single click. She let her head flop gratefully back into her pillow, exhaling softly in a satisfied victory, and trying to slow her rapidly pounding heart. Relaxing somewhat, she felt her breathing begin to even out once again, and focused on letting the elusive state of slumber finally take her.

"Don't fall back asleep, sweetie, or you'll wind up missing your flight."

Sam groaned, mumbled a mild curse and rolled over, pulling her pillow up over her head. She groaned again at Sarah's familiar touch as she gently ran a hand up Sam's back and tugged the pillow firmly from her grasp.

"You know I'm right," she said softly, kissing the back of Sam's shoulder. "You'd better get moving now, or you'll be sorry later."

Sam rolled back over to look at her girlfriend, touching her face in the morning dark, almost to reassure herself that Sarah was really there, next to her. She sometimes still couldn't believe it, even after all this time. Sam could almost see Sarah's bright blue eyes shining playfully at her in the coming dawn.

"Where do YOU get so much energy this early in the morning?" Sam asked grumpily, wrapping her arms around Sarah's waist and pulling her into a hug. "You been up eating your Wheaties already and not tellin' me?"

Sarah grinned and giggled quietly, kissing Sam lightly on the forehead.

"I always get excitable before a trip, you know that!" Sarah laughed as she wriggled out of Sam's grasp, planted a quick kiss on her lips and bounded out of bed. "Let's get moving!"

Sam moaned and sat up, rubbing morosely at her sleep-filled eyes. She shook her head and blinked angrily into the sudden glare from the bathroom light spilling into the room, her heart pounding in her chest.

"*You* are not *going* on a trip," she said, for what felt like the hundredth time. "*I* am going. *You* are staying. Got it?" Sam rolled out of bed and stood up, stretching. She could hear bits of her body popping in satisfaction as everything fell back into place. She yawned and scratched her head, wondering if she should actually bother doing anything to her hair, or just tug on a ball cap to wear on the plane. She looked up as Sarah appeared in the doorway, already brushing her teeth, and looking about as giddy as a kid at Christmas. That was not a good sign.

"I don't under-thand why you won't ju-tht let me go with you," Sarah mumbled around a mouthful of toothpaste. "I really think it'll be ea-thier than you think, and muth ea-thier with me there by your thide to thupport you." She ducked back into the bright light, and Sam could hear the water run in the sink briefly while she spit the toothpaste out and rinsed her mouth. Then she was back, grinning that special smile she had that melted Sam every single time.

"Besides," she smiled, "I really want to meet your sisters. I've heard so much about them, and I think now is the time." She turned more serious. "It's time, honey."

Sam shook her head, stomping around the bed as she grew more frustrated. She looked around for the bag she had packed the night before, checking to see if her ball cap was with it, just in case, then turned to face Sarah again, fully awake now.

"No, Sare, it's not time. It's really not. I mean," Sam backpedalled, seeing Sarah's face fall a bit in the light from the doorway. "I mean, it's not that I don't want you to meet them, or them to meet you. Jules will love you, trust me. But Em..." Sam faltered, unsure of what to say, as she felt

5

the panic swell up inside her again. "I just don't know what Emily will do. What she'll think. What she'll say." Sam crossed the room and gently took Sarah's face in her hands, looking into her blue eyes with as much sincerity as she could muster that early in the morning.

"Please understand," she begged desperately. "I will tell them about you. About us. I will. I'm just afraid that it'll get ugly, or something, and I really don't want you there to see that. I don't want any of that to fall on you. Okay?"

Sarah opened her mouth, looking like she wanted to say more, then closed it again, looking at Sam so intently that Sam dropped her eyes, unable to take any more scrutiny just then. She worried that there would be so much more of *that* to deal with later as it was, and could feel her earlier panic taking hold once again. Sarah's hands smoothed down Sam's wayward morning hair, and she tilted her head to kiss Sam lightly on the cheek.

"I think you're making a mistake." she said quietly. "But if you really don't want me there, then I guess I don't have a choice. I'm at least taking you to the airport, though, so go get ready. I'll go see if I can siphon a snack or two from the kitchen for you to eat on the way." Sam turned to watch her as she strode from the bedroom.

"It's not that I don't want you there..." she began, but Sarah was already gone. Feeling sullen, Sam flipped on the shower taps, and waited for the water to heat up. It was going to be a very long trip.

*   *   *

Sam let the hot water of the shower beat down on her as she inhaled deeply, trying to clear her head. Part of her wanted to just change her mind right then, and let Sarah come with her. It'd be so great to have her there, especially with Jules, because she already knew about the two of them and would be so excited to be able to finally meet Sarah. Sam smiled to herself at the image which sprang to her mind at the thought. She knew the two women would hit it off great and adore each other almost instantly. If it was just Julie that Sarah would be meeting, Sam would feel no hesitation whatsoever.

Emily, however, was another matter.

6

Her eldest sister had always seemed very critical of Sam. Em and Julie were closer in age, so they had often played together as kids, and hung out more socially as they got older and into high school. But where Julie had always made time to include Sam and do things together just the two of them, Emily had always seemed distant and unreachable. Sam had worshipped the ground Emily walked on, but no matter what Sam did, Em had always seemed to be above such things...things that her kid sister enjoyed, at any rate. Especially after their parents were killed.

Some rich kid on a bad drug trip had killed his friend, and then had crashed into their parents' car, killing them instantly, on Halloween when Sam was seven years old. She and Julie had returned to the house from trick or treating and the police were already there, delivering their devastating news of the accident to Emily who, at just a few months past her nineteenth birthday, was abruptly and tragically the adult of the house. That had been 25 years ago. And from that moment on, everything had changed.

Emily had graduated high school with Honours and was her class Valedictorian, but she immediately dropped out of University and took up a couple of part time jobs, in a valiant and mostly successful effort to keep her sisters together and in school. She got the house in their parents' will, but they hadn't had much else, and after the funerals were taken care of, there really wasn't much left to live on, so Em had taken it upon herself to see to it that they all stayed together and that the bills still got paid.

Julie had been a brilliant student, as well, and was on her way to walking in her sister's footsteps, but at fifteen, she had fallen apart the day their parents were lost. She'd barely managed to scrape through high school, and had stopped there, getting a job as a bartender in a local pub as soon as she turned nineteen. Now, at age thirty-nine, she had a failed marriage under her belt, no children, she was back living in the house they'd grown up in with her older sister, and was still tending bar for a living, while occasionally buffering the intermittent battles that continued to occur between Emily and Sam.

Emily, now forty-three, had never married, though Sam sometimes felt as though Emily had used the reason of having to raise her youngest sister as an excuse to not ever get back out in the world and live her own life. Instead, she seemed to want to control Sam's so she could

7

live vicariously through her, even though Sam always seemed to come up as a disappointment and failure in her sister's eyes. The two battled ferociously at times, particularly as Sam had grown through her teens. By the time she'd attended University, she had done so simply out of a desire to get away from home, rather than out of a drive to succeed or learn anything in particular. That was something which Emily, having given up her shot at higher education when she was in her prime, could not fathom at all. Samantha's seeming inability (or unwillingness, as it more likely seemed to Emily's eyes) to settle down and apply herself in school was not something Emily was able to tolerate. She'd worked hard for years so that at least one of her sisters could go on and make something of themselves, and her youngest sister had seemed to have had the best shot...and was coming up the shortest, bouncing around from school to school, course to course, and job to job in between, never making up her mind. To Emily, it all seemed like a grand waste of everyone's time, effort and money.

Sam, at thirty-two years of age, was now on her third attempt at a degree, having been unable to decide on anything long enough to declare a major and achieve the required number of credits in any of the fields she had tried so far. She'd landed at her current school on a whim, wanting to try her hand at journalism, but had quickly changed to creative writing when she'd discovered that it was a positive outlet for her to vent and purge anything she wanted or needed to, and have it actually graded favourably by her professors, rather than feeding on other people's angst ... other people's stories ... and garnering a lukewarm reception, at best. Sam had enough of her own angst; her own stories to tell. And she was good at it. From the time she'd turned in her first creative assignment, Sam knew it was where she wanted to be. The 'A' grade she'd received only further proved the point. Sam had finally found her niche. Julie had been thrilled, of course, but Sam had thus far been unable to tell Emily about her writing, afraid that her older sister would 'poo-poo' the idea as she had all the rest, thinking it was an even bigger waste of time and money because it wouldn't lead to any kind of job or lucrative salary in the field. Sam wanted Emily to be proud of her, and she finally had found a way to make her so, but was terrified that she wouldn't be, and so had kept it from her, letting Em continue to believe that Sam was studying journalism, instead. That had seemed disappointing enough to her sister, and creative writing would appear to be an even worse choice, but to Sam it was deeply personal, and profoundly effective. The grades and success so far alone had been well worth the wait. And then she had met Sarah.

The two of them had been standing next to each other in line for a summer course registration, back in the late spring. They had shaken hands and chatted while they waited, and for Sam it seemed there had been an instant connection. It wasn't until later that she found out Sarah had felt the same way. The two had become practically inseparable very quickly, and had opted to move in together once the fall semester began, a decision which thus far had made both of them extremely happy. They'd had a few of the same classes, but there were days that they really only saw each other in the evenings, and they had fallen into a comfortable routine of making dinner and watching TV, when there weren't assignments to work on, or books that needed to be read. The pair had become instantly comfortable with one another, something Sam had never experienced before, and often she had to blink and pinch herself to make sure it was actually real. Julie once said that, from what she could tell ("Never having met her", she'd always been quick to point out), Sarah was one of the best things to happen to Sam, and that they seemed to be good for one another. Sam couldn't agree more. Everything seemed to finally be falling into place. She was truly enjoying her life, maybe really only for the first time.

Samantha had told Julie, in a tearful confession years ago, about her attraction to other women. Jules had hugged and held her, telling her softly over and over that it was perfectly fine and natural and that she was still loved. Loved more, in fact. Jules had been awesome. Sam had made her promise, though, never to tell Emily, fearing that it would be the last straw, and that Em would disown her completely out of sheer disappointment and disgust. Julie had disagreed wholeheartedly, but thus far had kept her secret, as promised.

Sarah had been very understanding, as well, and had taken Sam home with her several times to meet her parents and younger brother over the course of the past several months. She'd wanted Sam to see what an open, accepting family could be like, and had begun gently encouraging her to have some faith in her own. And Sam desperately wanted to. She was feeling so much lighter lately...more than she could remember ever being before, and it did feel like it was getting to be time

9

to come clean with Emily. She wanted both of her sisters to meet Sarah and see how happy they were and be proud and happy for them...to see how amazing Sarah was, and to grow to love her as much as they loved their sister. Sam wanted that more than anything. She wanted to add Sarah to her family, as Sarah had added Sam to hers. She just...couldn't...yet. It all seemed so fragile to her...the sudden success at school, the happiness she'd found with Sarah...everything was going so well and Sam was terrified of ruining it somehow. Of losing it. She was afraid that if she let Emily in on the secrets most precious to her, that Em's disappointment - and perhaps anger and possible hatred - would somehow break the spell and have some darker reality crash down upon her, spoiling it all. Sam wanted to hold onto it, all of it, for as long as she could. If it was all a dream, Sam never wanted to wake up.

It's settled then, she thought resolutely to herself as she turned off the taps and stepped out of the shower, feeling her heart resume its panicked pounding once again. *Sarah can't come with me. Now is not the time. Nope, not the right time at all.*

Swallowing the sudden lump of disappointment that had risen in her throat, Samantha grabbed a towel and turned to face her reflection in the steamy mirror, still wondering what the hell she was going to do with her hair.

*   *   *

Julie Collins (it had been Turner-Collins for awhile, but she'd happily dropped the Turner part as soon as her divorce had finally gone through), flipped off her alarm and rolled reluctantly out of bed. She'd been awake for hours already, her nerves on edge for the coming day.

Padding across the carpeted floor of her bedroom, she pulled on a robe and strode quietly down the hall to the washroom. She closed the door behind her and flipped on the light, even as she heard the clinking of Trick's collar as he jumped from Emily's bed and headed down the hall toward her, thinking no doubt that it was time for his walk. Julie smiled to herself. *Not yet, buddy*, she thought. *Soon, but not quite yet.*

Emily had come up with the idea to get a dog several years after their parents had been killed one Halloween. Samie in particular had taken their death very hard, as she'd been so young when it had happened, and so, to help ease the pain that each recurring Halloween continued to bring them all, Em had decided that they should have a dog. A family pet. Something to mark the holiday with a happier memory, for a change.

Julie had gone with Emily to pick out the puppy on that Saturday morning while Samantha slept in, happy to avoid having to go to school on Halloween, for once. The two girls had searched carefully for what they hoped would be the perfect pet, one that would bring them all laughter and companionship and, perhaps most importantly, put a rare smile on their little sister's face. Having just turned 18, Samantha wasn't so little anymore, but the smile they sought was still just as rare as it had been after they'd first lost their parents. They'd been looking in secret, together and independently, for just over a week, and were determined on that particular day that they would not go home empty-handed. They looked at a couple of dogs that had made the short-list, and then headed to a new pet store in a nearby town for one last look before they made their decision.

As it turned out, the girls hadn't needed to go any further than that. They'd walked into the store, around a corner...and fell in love. Sitting alone and unafraid, watching the world outside his glass cage with affected disinterest hidden behind a wise face and intelligent eyes, was Trick. He was a 4-month-old shepherd-collie mix with brown and black fur and a small patch of white on his belly. He stood up as Emily and Julie approached, and began wagging his tail. They knew, from that moment, that they were all meant to be together.

The girls took him straight home, and woke Samantha up so that she could meet her new surprise right away. They'd wanted Sam to name the puppy, since she wasn't able to help pick him out, so that she could still feel involved in the process. It was one of the only things the three of them had done together, really, in recent memory. Samantha had tried to appear aloof at first, seemingly confused as to what her sisters were up to, and why they were trying so hard to include her all of a sudden.

But their enthusiasm was nearly as contagious as the puppy was adorable, and he and Sam had become fast friends. He was the family pet, but he was Samantha's dog, right from the start. They then treated

11

Halloween as his birthday, since that was the day he'd first joined their family. And Sam had named him Trick for, as they quickly found out, he was no treat. A training course or two later, Trick became a valued member of the household. But as a puppy, he more than earned his name in no-longer-identifiable, chewed-up former possessions and the occasional accidental surprises left around the house for the girls to find at their leisure. Sam once remarked that perhaps she should have just named him "OOOPS" and been done with it. But Trick was a fast learner, and was quite possibly Samantha's best friend. When she wasn't home, he happily and fairly divided his time between Emily and Julie, as needed. But whenever Sam was around, Trick was her constant companion.

Julie ignored Trick's soft scratch at the door, peering intently at her reflection in the mirror, instead. She ran her fingers through her shoulder-length, dark brown hair, and considered the fatigue she felt was showing in her clear blue eyes. Apart from a few smile lines around her eyes and the odd grey hair here and there, Julie had looked much the same in her late-thirties (okay, so she was almost forty, but who was counting?) as she had in her mid-twenties. Now, however, she felt that her years were beginning to show more and more with each passing day. Her face was becoming paler and more drawn, her hair thinner and more frail, with new lines and wrinkles seeming to appear overnight and growing deeper as the days wore on. In some ways, she was reminded of how she'd felt during her first rounds of chemotherapy treatment, as again, she was beginning more and more to look how she was feeling. And she knew it was only going to get worse from there.

Her plan, after taking Trick out for a walk, was to get in and out of her doctor's appointment as quickly as possible, then go and meet Samantha's plane when it landed. Judging by how badly she'd been feeling the past week and a half, Julie sensed that the news she was about to receive when she saw her oncologist later that morning would not be very good. The latest tests had been to see if there was a way to halt the spread of the disease after it had entered her glandular system, and Julie knew that, no matter what was confirmed today, she was going to be unable to hide the fact that the disease was back from her sisters any longer. Emily was already suspicious, she knew, and Sam would suspect something as soon as she got a good look at Julie later that afternoon. She couldn't keep it to herself anymore. Julie was going to have to tell both of them, and they were not going to like it. Just the fact that she'd kept it from them this long, Julie knew, was going to hurt them both deeply. And that was the last thing Julie had ever wanted to do.

Julie sighed at the sound of another light scratch at the door.

"Give me another minute, or two, Trick-ster, 'k?" she said in a low voice. "Let me throw something on first."

Smiling faintly at the sound of a forsaken *humpfh* as Trick gave up for the moment and camped outside the door to await her eventual emergence, Julie took one last look at her reflection and began carefully brushing her teeth, preparing as best she could for whatever the long day ahead would bring.

*   *   *

Emily Collins lay awake in the master bedroom; in what had once been her parents' bedroom a lifetime ago; listening to the sounds of the house, Trick's light snoring at the foot of the bed, and the restless pounding of her own heart. She knew she would soon have to get up and leave the calm, warm comfort of her bedroom sanctuary, to face the the stress and tasks of the coming day, but she wasn't ready to just yet. Not that she could sleep, anyway. Her mind whirled uncontrollably around the several issues she would have to deal with over the next 15 hours, or so, as it had been doing most of the night, her brief moments of restless sleep aside. Sleep or no, though, she was warm and comfortable and relished these last moments of relative peace as best she could. It was as if the world was holding its breath for an extra moment or two before allowing the dawn of a new day to wash over everyone aboard.

Emily heard Julie's door open, and felt the bed shake as Trick's head came up, alert and listening. A moment later, he jumped to the floor with a light thump and padded down the hall, trying to head Julie off before she reached the bathroom. Emily smiled to herself as she heard the door click closed and Trick's light follow-up scratch, as if to tell Julie that he was there, since she clearly hadn't seen him when she'd shut the door.

"Foiled again, huh, Trick-sie?" she whispered into the dark.

Emily rolled restlessly onto her side, listening to the sound of Julie running water in the washroom, and Trick's heavy sigh as he lay down to wait for her outside the door. She heaved a sigh of her own. Emily did not want this day to begin. She wished she could somehow skip it all together; fast-forward to later tonight, when all of the Thanksgiving grocery shopping had been done, when her sisters were both safely back at home under one roof, and when her own secret errand was finally accomplished and done. It seemed that this day in particular had gotten too big...there was too much packed into it, and it all threatened to overwhelm Emily before it had even started.

In her mind, she went over her mental list of things to get done throughout the day. Julie was picking Samantha up at the airport, so that was one thing, at least, that she didn't have to worry about. She tucked away the sudden uprising of nerves at the idea of Sam travelling by plane, knowing that it was a useless worry, but a worry nonetheless. Ever since their parents had been suddenly and tragically taken from them one Halloween (*by a reckless young man who had thought he could hide behind his parents' wealth, no matter what horrific crimes he'd committed*, Emily growled bitterly to herself), Emily had worried about her sisters every time they'd left the house. Particularly Samie-Sam, with whom the fear had become almost completely irrational at times. Emily feared losing another family member more than anything. For years, she'd wished that she could place them both in protective bubbles and keep them in the house, under her care and protection, for the rest of the their lives. Learning to let them go and live their own lives was one of the hardest things she'd had to do, and even now it was often still a struggle.

Even deciding to get Trick had been a huge issue on her part. Emily knew that a dog would not have the same life span as she and her sisters, and she greatly feared the effect losing a pet someday would have on all of them, and on Sam in particular, who was just never the same kid after their parents had been taken from them. Emily supposed none of them were the same after tragedy struck, but ever since that awful night, Sam had seemed...different. She had withdrawn into herself, and seemed to constantly be at odds with some invisible internal struggle she had going on. She'd had days where she'd been very needy and demanding attention and affection from both her and Julie, and other days where she wouldn't let anyone near her, when she seemed almost to be running from something, but without actually going anywhere.

On those days, only Trick had been allowed to accompany her on

14

whatever inner journey she was undertaking. Passing Samantha's bedroom door, Emily had often overheard bits of the tearful conversations and confessions her younger sister would sometimes have with the dog. As much as it tore her heart out to not be able to help; to not be allowed to go in there and take her sister in her arms and try to console her; to help her battle her inner demons in some way, Emily knew that disrespecting the girl's privacy was the worst thing she could do, and so she'd left her sister alone with her dog on those days, hoping against hope that Sam would someday be able to bring whatever she was facing back to Emily so that she could finally try to help somehow.

The day Samantha had first left to go away to school, Emily had been panic-stricken. She hadn't wanted to let on to Sam how difficult is was for her to let her go, lest it spoil the girl's apparent enthusiasm and excitement. She was, after all, the first of them to pursue higher education after high school, and Emily and Julie couldn't have been prouder if they'd raised her themselves. In a way, of course, they had. But while Jules had gushed with her unique and ultimately contagious brand of enthusiasm over the whole prospect, Emily had remained distant, not wanting to influence Sam's choices with her own senseless fears and misgivings. In the end, Samie had chosen a school that seemed to her as though it was practically on the other side of the continent, thus putting Emily's worries through the roof at the idea of not being able to see and somehow protect her youngest sister every day.

Julie had sensed the tension and sought to ease it as best she could, but Samantha had still been able to pick up on enough of it to take it the complete wrong way. It was one of the many, gazillion things Emily and Sam had fought about over the years. It felt to Emily as though the tighter she attempted to hang onto Sam, the more easily her sister would slip through her fingers, and drift further and further away with each battle. It broke her heart, but she was learning. Learning to let her go, and hoping each time that the kid would find her way back home.

Emily shook her head in the lightening dark. *Not a kid*, she scolded herself silently. *She's in her thirties now, for goodness sake! Stop thinking of her as a child!*

It was difficult sometimes, though. Whenever Emily looked at her youngest sibling, she was simultaneously struck by the dueling emotions she saw flitting like clouds of a coming storm across her giant blue eyes any time the two of them were in the same room. One part sadness and longing, one part anger and accusation, and one part abject fear. It was the same look she'd had in her eyes the night their parents had been killed, and it had grown to monumental proportions, at times, since then, often spilling out of her in uncontrolled fits of despair. Emily didn't know how to help her in those moments, either. All she could ever think to do was hold her until it was over, but often, and particularly as she had grown older, Samantha would simply not allow it. Usually Jules could calm her down, as Sam had nearly always let Julie get close to her, but there was some volatile trigger in the relationship between Emily and Samantha that Emily had yet to understand, let alone find a way to diffuse and move past somehow.

Emily rolled back onto her back, frustrated with her seeming inability to relax even one iota this morning. She would deal with her increasingly distant sister once she'd arrived back home. There was no point in worrying about it until then. There were other things she had to get done first. Like the horror of pre-holiday grocery shopping in an already over-crowded and nearly picked-clean superstore. Why, oh why, did she always wait until the day before to get all of this stuff done?

Because this time, at least, she'd needed an excuse to get out of the house for a few hours on her own, and she knew that, given the opportunity, Jules would do pretty much anything to avoid having to go along for that particular shopping trip. And Emily needed to be alone for it, so she'd suggested that Julie pick Samantha up at the airport, and she would take care of the grocery shopping ordeal on her own. Jules had jumped at the chance to not go with her, and hadn't questioned the fact that Emily had planned to be gone for most of the morning and mid-afternoon at all. In fact, she would be lucky to get back to the house before the girls returned from the airport, but she figured she could get enough food and seem disheveled enough to make it seem believable. And she would, after all, brave the horror of the holiday grocery-shopping ritual. It was just that she had something else to do, first. Something neither of her sisters had any idea about. And today would finally be the day; the last day she would ever have to have anything to do with this. It filled her with a sense of dread mixed with relief, all at the same time.

Emily heard Jules exit the washroom, and head back to her room,

16

presumably to throw on some warm-ish clothes and take Trick out for his walk. She could hear Trick follow along obediently, patiently awaiting his opportunity to get excited. Emily felt guilty about hiding this secret from her sisters, particularly Julie, as she'd shared pretty much everything else with her for as long as she could remember. As protective as Emily felt about Sam, she felt a certain comfortable companionship with her middle sister; even more so as they'd grown older and matured. They had fought through Julie's cancer several years ago, and saw her through into its eventual remission. Emily also knew something had gone horribly wrong in Julie's marriage, to the point where it had landed her in the hospital one night, but Jules had always avoided any questions, and so Emily had let it drop. She'd decided that her sister, whatever the specifics were, had a right to keep them to herself, and while Emily had made it clear that she was there should Julie ever change her mind and want to talk about it, she had ultimately backed off and just found contentment in the fact that Julie was now safely back at home. She'd been putting in some long hours at the bar in recent months, and often seemed over-tired and not as quick to smile as she had been, but Emily knew that her tendency to worry often had her jumping at shadows, so she'd learned to leave Julie alone, knowing she could come to her if she ever needed to.

Emily had always known that she could lean on Julie any time she'd needed to, as well. There were many times, when she was at her wits' end with Samantha, that Julie had provided immeasurable comfort to both of them, often acting as a buffer when the two girls needed a break from one another. Julie really was much closer to both of her sisters than either of them were to each other. They all depended on her, in so many ways. Sam had once called Julie the glue that held their family together, and Emily was quite certain that her young sister had been absolutely correct in that assessment. Julie was the perfect balance of humour, compassion, empathy, and intelligence, all wrapped up in one little package. She wasn't really short, per se; she was about average height, Emily supposed. But she and then even Sam had eventually grown to be that little bit taller, leading to the inevitable short jokes that Julie had always somehow managed to take in the the good-natured manner in which they were meant. Emily didn't know what they'd have ever done without Jules.

That alone was reason enough for her guilt over keeping the secret of secrets from both girls, but from Julie especially. Emily just was never sure how to tell them, as they'd both seemed to have moved on, whereas Emily could not. Not until she'd seen it through to its completion. They'd all closely followed the trial of the man accused of killing their parents, along with one of his own friends, that fateful night so long ago. By the time he had been sentenced, they'd all known his face; the man who'd taken everything from them. They had known that he'd killed his friend in a fit of drug-addled rage then, with his other friend (who'd turned witness and testified against him at this trial) had taken a vehicle in a desperate bid to disappear quickly from the scene of that crime, and crashed into their parents' car, nearly splitting the vehicle in two. He had then panicked again and the two of them had run off on foot. The girls all had known his name; it was forever burned into their minds as a symbol of what was lost. And once he was behind bars, sentenced for life, her sisters had managed, to a degree, at least, to let go and move on with their lives.

Emily, however, had not. She never told anyone, but she'd remained in contact with the officers who had been handling her parents' case, and she'd secretly and quietly attended every parole hearing that had come up over the past 25 years, and then some, hoping each time that he would be left to serve out the full of his sentence. Which he had. Until today. Today, the man who had stolen all of their lives simply by his selfish and arrogant carelessness, would be set free. And Emily would be there to witness it.

She heard Julie head quietly downstairs, Trick bounding along ahead of her, sensing that a trip to the outdoors was finally near. She listened as Julie pulled on a sweater and grabbed Trick's leash, knowing full well he wouldn't need it, then heard her close and lock the front door as she let them both out into the cold morning air.

By the time her alarm clicked, Emily was sitting on the side of her bed, and flicked the off switch before the alarm could even begin to sound. Wiping a hand across her forehead, she stood up and stretched, already weary from the coming day. Pulling on her bathrobe, she padded her way to the washroom and closed the door, mentally adding a couple of bottles of wine to the ever-growing grocery list in her distracted and worried mind.

18

~2~

Sarah Myles grinned to herself in the dark as she felt Samantha settle back into sleep mode next to her in the bed. *My girlfriend is impossible*, she smiled. *Can't even get up when she has somewhere she has to go!*

Sarah took a breath and exhaled slowly, then spoke aloud into the darkness, urging Sam awake. Rolling over, she wrapped both arms around her in a hug, then reached up to remove the pillow from Sam's head, kissing her softly on the shoulder as she did so. As Sam grumbled, Sarah struggled to contain her laughter. She never failed to find it amusing that the girl had such a hard time in the mornings. When they'd first gotten together, Sam was a restless sleeper at best, so it was quite understandable that she should struggle to make it upright the following day. She said she'd always had trouble sleeping, and Sarah had had a front row seat for that trouble - for the first few months, anyway. Eventually, as Sam relaxed more into the relationship, she seemed to sleep far more soundly with each passing night, so long as Sarah was next to her. Since they'd moved in together at the start of term, Sam and Sarah both were often getting a solid 7 or 8 hours each night. But despite the increased sleep times, Sam still hated the mornings. Often she fought with everything she had to avoid having to get up. On this morning especially, however, she would have no choice.

Sarah got up and threw on the bathroom light, knowing that would be a step in getting Sam mobile. She began brushing her teeth, but kept talking, keeping her girlfriend from dozing back off, despite the presence of light in the room. She knew they had to have this conversation again; that it was time to push Sam's seeming steadfastness on this particular issue once more before she left. Her mouth full of toothpaste, she delivered the line she knew would hold Sam's attention, and keep her from falling asleep any more that morning.

"I don't understand why you won't let me go with you." Sarah knew Sam was torn about taking the trip at all, let alone having Sarah go along with her, even though she wouldn't say so, and kept talking, ignoring the fact that they'd already had this conversation a dozen times since Sam had agreed to go be with her sisters for Thanksgiving weekend. The two girls had not been separated for even a full day since they'd first met and started dating, and she knew that a big part of Samantha wanted Sarah by her side when she told her sister that she was dating a woman. She seemed to be afraid more for Sarah's sake than her own, though, and so Sarah pushed, trying more and more to convince Sam that it was the right thing to do, and that it would be okay. She intended to push as much as she had to, in fact, as she became increasingly aware that a large part of her was desperate to be next to Sam for the weekend, no matter what issues or events might arise. Sarah suspected there was something more to her decision than Sam was letting on, and found herself suddenly was feeling very protective of her girlfriend. So, while Sam's anxiety over the trip rose, Sarah became more and more determined to not let her go alone.

As their conversation grew more heated, however, Sarah grew uncertain as to how she should proceed. She'd been so sure that she could convince Sam to let her go along for the weekend that she'd already bought a ticket for the flight. She could cancel it, of course, but that wasn't really the point. As her weekend departure date grew closer, Sarah sensed that Sam was more than just nervous - she was actually afraid. And as Sarah hadn't yet planned to take the trip with her, she could only assume that it was something about going home, about being with her sisters, that was frightening her. So Sarah had purchased a ticket, packed a bag, and told her own family that she would not be joining them for the weekend, after all. They all loved Sam, and understood Sarah's need to go meet her girlfriend's family, for a change.

The only trouble was, despite her obvious uncertainty, Sam ultimately was remaining steadfast in her decision. Sarah decided to back off for the moment, knowing she would have one more chance before Sam boarded to convince her to change her mind. She looked into Sam's huge blue eyes, so afraid and yet begging for her understanding, and let her off the hook - temporarily, at least - before heading downstairs to put together a small care package for what she hoped would be the journey *both* of them were about to undertake.

Samantha rode quietly in the car, barely saying anything the whole way to the airport. She felt miserable. A huge part of her wanted to ask Sarah to turn the car around, or to at least take back what she'd said earlier about not wanting Sarah to come with her. The truth was, she really did want Sarah to come, but she wanted to have already told Emily about her and have some idea as to how she would react when she found out. She wasn't sure that springing Sarah on her with Sarah *there* was such a good idea. If Emily freaked out, or worse, it would at best be a very uncomfortable weekend for all of them, Sam would wind up wishing she'd just stuck to her guns and not allowed Sarah to come along this trip, and possibly damage her relationship so close to its beginning, to boot. She had always felt that she should tell Em in person, and just deal with the fallout either on her own, or with Julie's help. Sarah shouldn't be subjected to whatever family drama arose as a result. She should come next time, after Sam had come clean with Emily, and once she knew better how Em would react.

But the fact was, Sam didn't want to go without Sarah. Her anxiety about going home had spiked to an all-time high, as it always did this time of year, and she didn't relish at ALL the idea of spending the holiday weekend apart from the one person who had the power to calm her. She also wanted them both to be able to spend time with each other's families, and not have to hide anything from anyone anymore.

Sam stared glumly out of the car window, watching with complete and utter disinterest as the landscape sped by, hardly daring to breathe while her mind and heart waged an internal war on one another. This was so dumb. She was so dumb. She had been so certain that she'd had it all figured out. That she knew what was best. Now, though, as she sped toward the fate she had chosen for herself, she was no longer sure at all. Sam closed her eyes and heaved a dejected sigh. She felt Sarah reach over and take her hand, giving it a reassuring squeeze. Sam squeezed back gratefully, and looked back out of the window.

There was no point in worrying about it now. It was too late to change her mind. They'd arrived.

Sam tapped her passport impatiently on her thigh and fidgeted with the clasp of her carry-on bag. Anything to avoid looking into Sarah's concerned blue eyes at that moment. She knew she had to say something, but she couldn't for the life of her think of what. Incredibly, Sarah took the reins, instead. She reached over and touched Sam's face, gently forcing her to look at her.

"Listen," she said quietly. "I need to tell you something. I don't want you to be mad..."

"I don't want you to go." Sam cut in quickly, then shook her head in frustration. "I mean, I don't want you to go home. I - I want you to come. With me. Home."

Sam's eyes dropped to the floor at the look of surprise on Sarah's face. What was she getting herself into now? Sarah's hands fell to her sides, and she hesitated a moment, as if deciding what to say next; how she should respond. She opted for the safer approach.

"Are you sure?" she asked. "I don't want you to do this just because I've been pushing you on it."

"No," Sam responded slowly. "No, I'm not sure, really. But I am more sure that I don't want to be far away from you this weekend, and...I don't know...maybe it'll be alright. Maybe if I go on ahead and you catch a later flight, or something, I can..."

"I already have a ticket." It was Sarah's turn to cut in. And Sam's shot at being surprised.

"What?" Sam stared at her girlfriend, not quite believing what she'd just heard. "You have a...a what now?"

"A ticket." Sarah smiled faintly, glanced to the floor a moment, then looked Sam square in the eye. "I already got a ticket. For this flight. It's what I was trying to tell you before." She faltered hesitantly, unsure what she should say next, and attempting to gauge Sam's reaction before she tried to continue. She decided again to play it safer, and give Sam the out, in case she needed it.

"I can cancel it." she said decisively. "I'll cancel it. I just...wanted

22

us to have the option, is all. I wanted you to know you could still change your mind. In case...you know...in case you wanted to."

Sam continued to stare at her silently, seemingly unable to speak.

"Please," Sarah pleaded quietly. "Please say something, honey. Tell me what you're thinking. Please." Sarah badly wanted to reach over and take Sam's hand, touch her face, hug her...anything to take that look of disbelief off of her face, but she stood her ground and didn't move, waiting instead to see what Sam would do; how she would react.

What seemed like hours, but were really only a few seconds, stretched out between them. Sarah held her breath, waiting.

"I love you." Sam breathed. Sarah blinked. She had definitely not been expecting that. She blinked again, trying to clear the buzzing in her ears.

"I'm sorry...what did you just say?"

Sam inhaled deeply, then exhaled very slowly, gazing at Sarah steadily the whole time.

"I said I love you," she repeated softly. "I love you and I want you to come home with me and meet my stupid sisters and have whatever disastrous Thanksgiving feast and family drama we can cook up and I want you to be there. With me. Us. Together. Please." Sam smiled then, and suddenly Sarah could breathe again. She wiped her eyes at a sudden tear that threatened to spill unbidden down her cheek, and nodded, finally cracking a grin herself.

"Okay, then, honey love. Let's get moving. I have a bag to salvage from the car and we have a plane to board!" She grabbed Sam's hand and pulled her into a tight hug. "I love you, too, you know," she whispered over Sam's shoulder. To her happy surprise, Sam laughed lightly.

"Yeah, yeah, I know," she winked. "Just remember who said it first."

*   *   *

23

Julie flopped gratefully onto the cold park bench and stretched her legs out, giving her aching feet and legs a break. Her appointment had not lasted long. Nor had it gone very well. *Spread*, they had said. Amid a stream of medical phrases, only that word, and *inoperable*, had managed to cut through the babble to her level of understanding. In a daze she had stood up, lifted her coat from the chair, and walked out of her doctor's office. For the time being, those two words were all she had needed to know. And so she had left.

When she hit the sidewalk, the sounds of the street - the traffic and all of the people going about their daily lives - had been too much for her to bear. It all felt too loud and way too damn fast. Julie had started walking, her feet moving along the pavement, gaining speed with every step. Until suddenly she was running. Without direction, without purpose, without thinking, Julie ran.

And found herself in the park, where she stopped running, as suddenly as she had begun, and seated herself on the nearby bench, out of the way, to gather her thoughts and try to pull herself back together somehow.

That was it, she knew. She would have to tell her sisters now. She wasn't sure which would upset them more, that she had such terrible news to share, or that she hadn't shared any of it before now. She wiped absently at an unchecked tear sliding down her cheek. She didn't know what to do.

Julie inhaled deeply, catching a hint of fall in the air. The leaves were all turning colour, and many had already fallen to crunch underfoot as people strolled by. In the playground nearby, two young girls chatted together while playing on the swings, while three boys tried to build a giant leaf pile that would inevitably be leapt into with reckless abandon. Julie found herself smiling as she watched them. She used to love playing like that with Sam when she was little. Emily had often been 'too old' for such things, but even she couldn't resist a good leaf pile.

The same had gone for tobogganing. All three girls had loved the feeling of flying headlong down a steep hill through the snow; tree branches and frozen twigs flashing past as they'd hurled by. When Sam had been much smaller, Emily and Julie had padded her snowsuit with whatever else they could find...sweaters, socks, extra long-johns. They had pumped her up to look like she was attending a family reunion with the Michelin Man, and took her out to the big hill for the first time.

There had been a fresh snowfall the night before, and a new trail had needed to be cut. Usually Emily and Julie had taken turns or, more often, had gone best two out of three in Rock, Paper, Scissors, to determine who would have the honour. They had to give that one up on the coldest days, since Paper and Scissors looked much the same when covered with mittens. But on this particular day, to celebrate Samantha's induction into their tobogganing ritual, the girls had agreed to send her down the hill first.

And they'd gone with the saucer as the toboggan of choice.

They had settled Sam into the aluminum disc, and instructed her to hold on tight to the handles located on each side. Sam, wide-eyed and rosy-cheeked, had obeyed with utmost seriousness. Emily had taken one side, Julie was on the other, and together they swung Sam lightly back and forth, counting as they went.

"One! ... Two! ... ... Two and a half!! ... THREEEEE!!!"

They released their younger sister in unison, propelling her the first several feet down the hill and laughing as they'd watched the saucer gain momentum. As it began to spin, Sam squealed in terrified delight, mouth open nearly as wide as her huge blue eyes. From the top of the hill, she had appeared still so small to Julie then, even with her puffed up snowsuit, her pompom-toqued head swirling ever closer to the bottom of the new trail she was blazing all by herself.

The saucer started on another rotation, and Julie caught a glimpse of Sam's face as she neared the bottom of the hill. Suddenly, though, she and the saucer hit something solid at top speed, flipped backwards and landed in a heap in the snow. Emily and Julie had continued laughing, applauding their little sister's spectacular stunt. When Sam didn't make a move to get up, however, the older girls had glanced fearfully at one another, and turned to run headlong down the hill toward their fallen sister.

Emily had reached her first, skidding to a stop in the snow and falling to her knees next to Samantha. The child was lying on her back, the saucer partially covering her small head. Slowly, gently, Emily pulled the saucer aside, and gazed down at her sister. Sam's face was a darker shade of red than they had ever seen before, her mouth still open, and her eyes squeezed shut. Emily laid a hand on her chest, and bent over her more closely. Julie stood on her other side, watching in horror, unsure of what to do.

Suddenly Sam inhaled deeply...and then laughed. A deep, from the belly, bellowing guffaw that echoed across the field. Her arms crossed her abdomen, her knees came up in a curl, and the girl *laughed*. Harder than they'd ever seen before or since. Samantha's initiation to the realm of tobogganing was complete. She was in love.

That had been a near perfect day for the three of them. It was one of the only times they'd been truly and happily together.

Julie chuckled aloud at the memory, and then jerked herself back to the present. The afternoon was getting on, and Sam's plane would be landing soon. She had to get to the airport to pick her up, then get home in time to maybe help Emily put the groceries away so that she could use the time to work up the courage to give them her devastating news.

Julie sighed and got to her feet. What she wouldn't have given for another day on the hill, laughing with her sisters. Sometimes she worried that none of them would ever laugh like that again. She checked her watch and started back in the direction of the parking lot where she'd left her car, silently tucking her happy memories away, to be called upon some other time.

*   *   *

Emily took a long drag on her cigarette and exhaled slowly, watching the smoke plume and slip out through the cracked window of her car. She was starting to get cold, but it barely registered. Her mind was far away, and right there, all at once. Across the road, the prison gate stood closed, indifferent to the world around it, awaiting its next opportunity to turn someone away, allow someone access to its guarded interior, or, in the case Emily was waiting for, to let someone out.

She inhaled once more from her cigarette, listening as the last of it burned away in the cold, silent air inside the car, and flicked it from the window to land in the soft wet leaves in the ditch next to her car. Glancing around, she wondered if that could be grounds for arrest. *How ironic would that be?* Emily thought with a self-effacing smirk. *That would be just my luck, really.*

She rolled the window the rest of the way up and reached to rub the back of her neck. She would be glad when this was all over. It seemed like this burden had been with her forever, and as relieved as she hoped she would feel when it was done, Emily secretly wondered how she would go on without it. This darkness had been a part of her for so long, she almost wasn't sure who she was without it. Pressing her fingers to her temples, she closed her eyes against the headache threatening to take hold. *So long,* she thought to herself. *So much time, gone. And now, suddenly, it is nearly done.*

A knock on the window snapped Emily out of her reverie. Her mind barely registered the police uniform before a glance into a familiar face made her eyes widen in recognition. Blushing suddenly, she smiled awkwardly and rolled her window down, catching her breath in apprehension as she did so.

"Hi...Officer..." she stammered, unable to meet the brown eyes that were gazing at her when they were this close up. "I was just...um...sorry, am I doing...something wrong?" Emily suddenly and fervently hoped he hadn't just witnessed the cigarette episode.

Officer Ryan Mullen watched her intently for a moment, and Emily's heart skipped a beat. Then his face broke into a grin, causing her to relax almost instantly.

"Hey, there, Ms. Collins," he smiled. "Fine day for a drive, I see."

Emily reached up to unconsciously twist a lock of hair nervously around her finger. Why did he make her feel so fumbly and awkward all the time? She forced a tight smile that she prayed at least looked somewhat convincing.

"Emily," she said, shaking her head. "We've known each other long enough that I think it's long past time you just called me Emily."

27

Officer Mullen ducked his head and leaned an elbow on her window. His smile was disarming, as were his soft and friendly brown eyes. *Rather like a big puppy*, she thought to herself, smiling further.

"Well, okay, Emily," he said, his grin widening. "I guess you've got a point, so I'm going to have to insist that you call me Ryan." The pair chuckled awkwardly for a moment, and Emily sheepishly peered up at him, unsure of what to say next.

"So...what seems to be the problem, Offi - Ryan?" she asked. Ryan looked around, then jerked his thumb back over his shoulder, at the prison gate across the street.

"Now, I know why you're here, and believe me, I understand..." he began. Actually, Emily was fairly certain he did *not* understand, but out of everyone who knew her, he was likely to be the one who could come the closest to knowing what her motivations were in this, so she let him have it. Ryan had been there from the beginning, she knew. As a rookie cop, he had turned up at her door with his partner on that horrible Halloween night so long ago. He'd been there all through the trial, always nearby in case she or the girls had needed anything. And he had kept her up-to-date on the convicted's parole hearings, sitting with her while the man's fate was decided time and again. Officer Ryan Mullen had also done her an enormous favour once upon a time; one that could never be repaid. He'd been a tremendous support to her over the past 25 years, and suddenly Emily wasn't at all sure what she would do without him, either.

Right now, however, she appeared to be ignoring him, as he had just said something that she, in her absentee mind, hadn't caught a word of, and now he was looking to her for some sort of reaction. Unable to think of something on the spot that would cover every possibility, she gave up, and opted to keep it simple, instead.

"I'm sorry...what?"

Officer Ryan blinked a moment, then smiled in that crooked, charming way of his, as though bemused by some inner thought. After a moment, he grew more serious.

"Emily, we both know what day this is," he said in a low voice, "and we also both know, that you can't be here." He looked at her pointedly, and waited. Emily's heart skipped a beat, and she suddenly felt nauseous. She couldn't just leave; not yet. She wasn't ready yet.

"Please," she began, "I know what you're thinking..."

Just then, the prison gate swung open, and a dark blue car pulled up to the roadway across from where she was parked. Squinting into the sun, Emily could tell that there were two figures in the front seat, but wasn't able to make either of them out very clearly. Ryan stood up from his perch at her window, and turned to look, as well. Emily held her breath. This was it; she could feel it.

The car's left-hand turn signal came on, and the driver waited as a couple of cars passed by, watching for an appropriate gap in the light oncoming traffic. Emily sat as still as a stone, staring transfixed at the simple, midnight black sedan just a few yards away from where she'd parked. The air around her seemed to hum. Everything...time itself...seemed to pause, stretching the moment out to the point where she was unsure that she could bear it. This *had* to be it. It just had to be.

All of a sudden, the driver got the break he'd been waiting for, and the car eased forward into its turn. The sun's bright reflection bounced briefly off of the car's windshield, and Emily was momentarily blinded. But as it rolled forward, completing its turn and beginning to accelerate off down the road, she saw him.

He was sitting on the passenger side, wearing a black leather jacket over a grey cable knit sweater. A light stubble covered his chin, and his short dark brown hair was flecked with gray. He looked much older, more drawn and weary than she'd seen him before. He looked small, uncertain, perhaps even sad and somewhat afraid.

And he was looking right at her, his grey eyes already widening slightly in recognition.

Everything seemed to move in slow motion. Emily and the man who had stolen her life stared at one another, each watching closely to gauge what the other might do, if anything. She craned her neck slightly, trying to get a better look; trying to squeeze everything possible from this one impossible moment. The car began to pick up speed, and the man had turned a little in his seat, seeming also to be unable to release the moment quite yet. His hand came up into view and froze in the air, as if he had been about to wave and then thought the better of it. Instead, his head bobbed in a quick, silent nod of acknowledgment and respect...and then he was gone; the sedan having continued on along the road, and was now already nearly out of sight.

Emily sat frozen, staring down the road, even though the car had already vanished from view. Lungs burning, she vaguely realized she still hadn't drawn a breath, and suddenly gasped, grateful for the air and that the brief but unpleasant spell she'd been under had finally been broken. Becoming dimly aware that Ryan was crouched back down beside her window, she glanced over at him momentarily, then quickly looked away, completely unable to think of anything she could say. Seeming to sense her discomfort, he broke the silence, instead.

"Are you okay, Emily?"

The kindness and genuine warmth in that simple question, in his simple words, made her heart skip another beat. She wiped at a tear that had slipped suddenly down her cheek, and glanced at him again, both surprised and somehow comforted by the look of sincere concern she saw on his face as he gazed at her, quietly. She started to shake her head, and then it was upon her, washing over her in a wave of despair and anguish, completely unchecked for the first time since her parents had been killed. All of the years she'd spent putting her own needs and wants aside so that her sisters, her beautiful sisters, could have something more, if they'd wanted it. All of the dreams that had been shattered. All of the guilt she'd felt at having had such wonderful parents for so long, losing them, and then being really the only parent that Samantha would really remember. Emily wept. She wept for the lost years. She wept for her sisters. She wept for herself. She wept for her lost parents, who'd been taken too suddenly and too quickly to ever know how truly loved and appreciated they had really been. And she wept for the man who had, in one fateful stroke,

30

destroyed his own life and youth in the same instant as he had destroyed all of theirs. Emily wept until there was nothing left inside of her to come out.

And, once her tears had finally stopped flowing, as she took her first shaky, cleansing breath, she realized that his arms were around her...that they had been since she'd first begun. Ryan had simply sat and held her, not saying anything, not asking anything of her, as Emily had just finally let it all go. She felt herself blushing again, and was surprised, glancing quickly at him as he stood up again, to see that he was, too. She decided to put an end to the awkward silence before it could start.

"Look, Ryan," she began earnestly, "I can't be here. It's against policy, or something, I think. So I should just go." She started the engine, while he took a step back. He smiled again, hesitantly at first, then let it spread across his entire face.

"Well, ma'am, if you say so..." he grinned while he mimed tipping his hat.

"I do." Emily put the car into gear, and began to roll up the window. "And Officer?"

His eyebrows raised in question.

"Yes, ma'am?"

"First of all, thank you for helping me. With the car, I mean, of course." He nodded, still smiling.

"And second, please don't ever call me 'ma'am'...or I am going to have to hurt you."

Before he could summon a response, Emily turned the car around, winked, and drove back the way she had come. Checking the rearview mirror, she saw him still standing in the middle of the road, watching her go. Sighing, she turned her mind forward to the hellish grocery shopping trip ahead, and the uncertain upcoming reunion with her youngest sister. She glanced in the mirror again just before Officer Mullen disappeared

31

from view.

"Goodbye, Ryan." she whispered to the reflection. "And thank you. For everything."

With that, Emily pressed the gas pedal down a little further, and headed back into town.

~3~

Duncan Rolston turned back to face the front of the car, watching in the rear-view mirror until the vehicle he'd seen parked behind them disappeared from sight. He had, of course, recognized the officer standing next to that car immediately; he'd seen him many times over the past 25 years.

It had taken him a moment, however, to recognize the woman inside the vehicle. He'd seen her many times, as well, but mostly only in the beginning. It had been a very long time since he'd seen her last, but despite how the years in between had aged and changed her, he knew instinctively who it was behind that wheel. Smiling grimly to himself, he realized he was not at all surprised. He supposed, deep down inside, that he'd actually expected her to be there, watching him as he took his first steps of freedom.

Duncan thought back to the last time he'd seen Emily Collins. He'd been used to seeing her at his trial, and then at his subsequent appeal hearings; whenever the public was permitted, at least. Duncan had stopped being surprised to see her long ago.

Except for that last time. He had certainly not been expecting that.

The last time Duncan Rolston had seen Emily Collins, it was because she had come to the prison and assaulted him.

*   *   *

Duncan wiped a hand across his forehead, leaned his head back and closed his eyes, forcing his breathing to slow and return to its regular rhythm. He imagined that no one had been more surprised that day than he had been, watching as she, of all people, crossed the room toward him and took a seat across the table from him. She'd appeared apprehensive,

33

but resolute, and looked to be the same level of exhausted as he had felt.

It had been a beautiful sunny day, not long after his most recent appeal had been turned down. He'd no longer really been holding out hope that the appeal process would ever work for him but, at his attorney's insistence, he'd continued with it, anyway. Collins had been present at the courthouse during his appeal, of course, but the last thing he'd ever expected was to see her sitting so close to him, looking at him so intently that he'd quickly become uncomfortable. Duncan Rolston did not like being made to feel uncomfortable, and he had instantly brought his guard up, attempting instead to go on the attack.

Before he could get more than two words out, however, Emily Collins surprised him yet again. Quick as lightning, she'd pulled a slightly wrinkled paper from her coat pocket, and slammed it down on the table with such sudden force that his words were choked off in his throat. It was a photo...a casual family portrait, taken in a grassy field somewhere, with each person sitting on or crouched around a large log, so long dead and fallen that the sun had bleached it white over the years. The breeze was gently blowing their hair back from their faces as they'd squinted into the bright sun. The five faces smiling at him out of that photograph had betrayed not a care in the world. But Duncan had known that image was from the past; a past that none of them could or would ever reclaim.

A past he had taken from them.

The photo had seemed to be fairly recent as, despite how grief and fatigue had taken their toll, Emily Collins did not appear to be very far removed from the age of her photographed self. Duncan's eyes had moved from one face to the next, taking in the three blue-eyed daughters - the youngest one, twiddling a blade of grass between her fingers, still just a child - and then had reluctantly and nervously moved to the parents. The woman, their mother, appeared natural and carefree, her dark hair pulled back into a loose ponytail. Sylvia Collins had sported an easy smile and appeared quietly maternal, with an arm draped loosely around the shoulders of each of her two youngest daughters.

Holding his breath, Duncan had then looked directly into the face of the Collins girls' father, the only man in what had once looked to be a beautiful family. His hair was a slightly lighter brown than the girls', but he had the same wide, sparking blue eyes as his daughters, and the intelligence in those eyes seemed to leap from the photo and bore right to Duncan's core. He had, thus far, managed to avoid looking directly at pictures of the man, but now he found himself trapped, and seemingly unable to look away.

He closed his eyes against the sudden memory of that night as it welled up unbidden within him, and pushed the accompanying panic to the back of his mind. Duncan swallowed, his mouth suddenly very dry, and opened his eyes again to find Emily Collins staring back at him; a strange, unreadable expression on her face. He cleared his throat, forcing a countenance of what he hoped was casual indifference to his face, and spoke quietly.

"What do you want from me?"

Emily appeared momentarily taken aback by the sudden directness of his question, but she recovered quickly, and an air of cold steel fell over her once again as her eyes, so much like her father's, gazed searchingly into his. He held his breath, awaiting her response. After a moment, her eyes broke to the picture, and she tapped a finger, gently, on first her mother, and then her father.

"These are my parents," she began in a quiet voice of icy calm. "I know you have heard over and over of the kind of people they were; the kind of people you took from the world before their time. I think you've heard so much that you stopped listening long ago, so I am not here to talk about them this time. Instead, I thought I would come here to talk about who you took them *from*."

Duncan groaned inwardly and rolled his eyes. He sat back in his chair and, realizing that he didn't have to sit there and listen to anything she had to say, began to push himself to his feet. Strong hands on his shoulders forced him back.

"Sit down," an authoritative voice commanded from behind him. He turned to glare up at the officer standing there, and was not at all surprised to see that it was *him*, Mullen, the First Man On The Scene the night of the accident. It seemed to Duncan that, ever since that night, wherever Emily Collins went, Officer Ryan Mullen was never very far behind. Of course he would want to be here to help the girl spring her little guilt trap on big bad guy, Duncan Rolston. Feeling his ire rise up in him, Duncan took a deep breath and released it, reminding himself of what would happen if he were to anger any of the officers on duty, trap or no. Sighing in resignation, he collapsed against the back of his chair again, clasping his hands on the table in front of him, and pasted a properly chastised expression onto his face.

"Fine," he growled. "Have at it, then." Emily Collins shook her head, a sad smile on her face. She seemed disappointed.

"I had a feeling you wouldn't listen to anything I had to say, anyway," she said in that same icy calm voice. "So instead, I want to hear what you have to say." Duncan blinked at her.

"Excuse me?" He licked his lips as his eyes darted nervously around the near-empty room. Officer Mullen had strolled over to the far wall where he could watch without intruding further. No one else was within earshot. It was, for the most part, just the two of them. Emily leaned forward in her chair, and whispered to him almost conspiratorially.

"I want you to tell me what happened, what you remember." She sat back. "I want you to tell me everything."

Duncan gaped at her a moment, then chuckled quietly. He shook his head.

"Look, no offence, lady, but why in God's name would I ever even remotely entertain the idea of doing such a thing?" Emily raised an eyebrow and held his gaze steadily.

"Because you are going to be here, in this prison, for a very long time. Nothing you can say now is going to change that. You'll tell me because I might just be the only person left on this planet who still wants to hear your side of things, before I leave you here to rot, all alone, in your

36

cell. And you'll tell me everything, not because you owe it to me, or to them," she said, her finger again tapping each person in the photograph on the table between them, "but because the truth of what you have done will otherwise sit there inside of you, and eat away at you until there is nothing left of you to see." She sat back in her chair again and eyed him calmly.

"You'll tell me because, deep down inside, you want to. You know you need to tell *someone* all about it, and the only person left who cares to listen to you at all...is me."

Duncan stared at her, unsure what to say. His eyes flicked back to the photo in front of him. That Emily Collins, the one in the photo, was smiling contentedly, very different from the girl - the woman - in front of him now. Her sisters were also grinning away, the little one twirling the blade of grass almost as though she were waiting expectantly for him to speak. Arthur and Sylvia Collins, smiling happily, suddenly appeared to be waiting as well, their expressions forever frozen in time, as the moments between he and the Emily here and now, slowly ticked by. His heart hammered in his chest as he considered what to do. His eyes met those of Arthur Collins once again, and in that instant, Duncan knew that Emily had been right. He did need to talk about his memory of what had happened that night. The truth would not set him free, he knew, but it also couldn't do any further harm if it were to come out now. He no longer wanted to be the only one carrying the burden of what had really happened; what he had really done. The only trouble in telling her, even now, was that Emily Collins was not going to like what she was about to hear. No, she was not going to like it at all.

Sighing again, Duncan took a deep breath, and began to speak.

~4~

Samantha was nearing full on panic mode when she felt Sarah take hold of her hand and give it a firm but gentle squeeze.

"Babe, you have got to *breathe*," she whispered. "You are freaking out way too much. It's going to be fine. Just relax. And breathe, okay?"

Sarah nodded rapidly and tried to mentally pry her shoulders from under her ears back down to where they belonged.   She was marginally successful, at most. Sarah chuckled quietly next to her.

"Seriously, hon, take a deep breath. Let it out slowly. Everything is going to be okay. It will."

Sarah seemed pretty emphatic. Sam was less sure. Sam was leaning the other way entirely, actually. This was a mistake. She didn't even know anymore exactly what the mistake had been, whether it was in letting Sarah come with her, or whether it was in going back home at all. She'd never wanted a plane to turn around so badly in all her life. Instead of turning back, however, the pilot had just come on to announce that they would soon be landing. From that moment on, Samantha had been fairly certain that she was about to throw up.

From the corner of her eye, Sam saw Sarah abruptly turn in her seat, facing her full on. She reached across, grabbed Sam's other hand, and pulled, trying to get Sam to turn and face her, too. Sam couldn't meet her girlfriend's eyes. She looked around nervously, trying to figure out what was going on. Sarah looked at her intently for a moment, then inhaled deeply, and let it out slowly.

"OK," she began quietly. "That is *enough*. You are freaking out for no rational reason that I can see. So let's get to the bottom of it now, before we land, because you're making me feel like this is about me being here,

38

even though you ended up asking me to come. So let's start there." She paused, and wet her lips briefly before she spoke again.

"*Is* that what this is about? Do you not want me here? Do you want me to just get back on the plane and head back to school for the weekend, instead of coming home with you to meet your sisters? Would you be better off, feel better, if I just left? If I wasn't here?" She grew quiet then, watching Sam for a reaction. Waiting for some kind of answer. Hoping it would be different from what she feared it was. Sam looked at her then, her blue eyes betraying a hint of the anxiety she was feeling. What had she just said? Would Sam be better off if she wasn't there? That part was easy to answer.

"Absolutely not." Sam replied without hesitation. "I want you there, with me. I always want you there. I don't know where I would be without you. You know that."

"Then what is it?" Sarah asked. (That part wasn't so easy to answer.) "What, really, has got you so worked up right now? Are...are you afraid I'm going to embarrass you, or something? Are you afraid they'll hate me? Maybe?"

"Oh my God, Sarah, no! I feel so proud and lucky to...*hate* you? They're not going to hate you! They'll *love* you! They'll see how much I love you, and how amazing you are and they'll just love you, I know it." And she really did know it. Suddenly, Sam had never been quite so sure of anything before in her life. She pictured introducing Jules to Sarah when she picked them up at the airport. Jules would be giddy and ridiculous and awesome. Sam imagined the three of them laughing all the way home in the car together, getting caught up, singing along loudly, and badly, to cheesy songs on the radio. Just enjoying being together.

Then they would get home and...Emily would be there. Sam felt her brief moment of levity deflate within her.

"It's Em," she said quietly. "I'm just afraid. I don't know what she'll think. I feel like this will just be one more thing about me that's....wrong. That's a disappointment to her. She's not going to be mad, or hate me, or anything like that, at all...but I almost wish she would. Because I'd much prefer that to feeling like I've let her down...again. I'd take her anger over her disappointment in me any day." Sam's gaze dropped to the floor. She felt very tired all of a sudden.

Sarah sat quietly for a moment, considering, then cleared her throat, and reached up to take Sam's face in her hands.

"Listen to me, Samie-Sam." Their eyes locked and, satisfied that she had Sam's attention, she continued. "Now, I don't know your sisters, least of all Emily, because you talk about her so rarely. But you said she pretty much raised you, right?" Sam nodded, her eyes filling with tears. "Well, from what I can tell, you turned out to be a pretty amazing woman, which tells me that, not only must she have done something right..." Sarah wiped a tear off of Sam's cheek with her thumb, and leaned in a little closer, her face now just inches away, filling all of Sam's now-blurred vision. "...but that she must also love you very, very much. Because amazing people don't just happen every day. And she doesn't seem to be some sort of idiot, which tells me she knows the kind of gift that you are, and that she couldn't be anything but proud of you. If she didn't have faith in you, and love for you, she could have walked away, and not have chosen to keep you close to her all those years, right?"

Sam shook her head and pulled back a bit in her seat, feeling like a child but suddenly unable to stop crying just then.

"No...she didn't have a choice. She was stuck with me. She had no choice...they died and she was the oldest and...and she just had to. She had no choice...I ruined everything for her."

Tears flowing freely now, Sam buried her face in her hands. Sarah's arms were around her then, rocking her gently and rubbing her back. Her voice whispered in Sam's ear as she stroked her hair.

"No, sweetie, you've got it all wrong. She didn't need to drop out of school and get a job to take care of you and Julie and keep you all together. She didn't have to do that. She chose it, because she wanted to. She chose you, because she loves you, and because you're an important part of her life. She chose to keep you close because you're her baby sister." Sarah paused, waiting for Sam to catch her breath for a moment. Sam shook her head sadly.

"No, you don't understand, not with Em," she stated with a quiet sigh. "She's so brilliant, you don't know. She could have gone anywhere, done anything. She could have been anyone she wanted to be. If it weren't for me." Sam choked down a sob. "She gave everything up to take care of me after our parents died. Everything. Her whole life..." Tears continued flowing unchecked down her face. Sam didn't care anymore; she needed to finally get this out. Not everything, not even close. But this much, she needed to be able to say right now. She needed Sarah to understand. She looked at her girlfriend then, sitting quietly, watching her; giving her the room she needed without actually pulling away. Sam gazed at her a moment, overwhelmingly grateful and once again in a state of disbelief that she could have gotten so lucky as to have someone like Sarah in her life at all. Sam took a deep breath, and began again.

"She gave up everything. For me, you understand?" Sam waited for Sarah's nod before continuing. "She and Jules could have probably gotten by okay, if it weren't for me. If it had just been the two of them..." She shook her head again. "And what am I?" Sam whispered. "Em gave up her whole life so that I could have one...and look at me. I haven't done *anything*. What am I? I'm nothing. Not compared to what she could have been; to what she could have done. Is it any wonder that she's so disappointed in me? She gave everything up...for nothing..." Sam broke down again, but this time Sarah wasn't having any of it. She took a hold of Sam's face again, making sure she had her full attention once again.

"You stop that right now," she scolded softly. "You are NOT nothing. I know it, Jules knows it, and Em knows it, too. The only one who feels that way; the only one who doesn't know it, is you." Sarah smiled her special secret smile, reserved only for Sam in moments when they were completely alone. The crowded plane full of holiday travelers had disappeared for the moment. Sarah leaned forward, still smiling.

"You are *not* here to live her life for her. You are here to live *yours*. Stop comparing yourself to your sisters. They love you, *both* of them. As do I, by the way. And no one thinks you aren't worth what was given up in order to give you a chance. You just don't see yourself at all the same way the rest of us do, so we'll have to work on that. But in the meantime, you can rest assured that one basic truth is about to come to pass."

Sarah looked deep into Sam's eyes, and said exactly what she'd needed to hear. "From the moment...the very *instant*...that Emily meets

41

me, and see's how happy you make me, she'll be so proud of you. Because I'm just that awesome."

Sam stared at her a moment, sniffling, then burst into giggles. Sarah grinned, and gave her a devilish wink.

"You disagree?" she asked, pretending to be hurt. "You don't think I'm that awesome?"

"Oh hon," Sam laughed, brushing the last of her tears away with the back of her hands, "I think you are all kinds of awesome...and more." The girls kissed one another, still giggling, and sat back in their seats.

"I'm a dork." Sam stated. "I'm nervous, but...I guess it's possible it might go all right. Because you are made of awesome, naturally."

"You are a dork," Sarah agreed. "And everything will be great. Because I am made of awesome." She grinned over at Sam and ruffled her hair. "You're such a good little learner!"

"Shut it." Sam said, feigning annoyance. "This plane just ain't big enough to hold that expanding head of yours, so please try and tuck some of it away, would ya?" The girls laughed again, then grew quiet as the seatbelt sign came on, and the announcement was made that their descent had begun. Sam reached over and took Sarah's hand again.

"I love you, Sare", she said quietly. "Thank you...for everything."

Sarah lifted her hand to her lips, kissed the back of it, and gave it a gentle squeeze.

"Any time, hon. And I love you, too." She gave Sam a quick wink out of the corner of her eye. "Now. Let's go get this thing over with so that we can RELAX, for a change!"

Sam smiled and gazed out the window. For the first time, she thought they may actually be able to do just that.

*   *   *

Julie checked her watch for the 47 millionth time in the past fifteen minutes, then stared up at the Arrivals board again. Samantha's plane had landed a good twenty minutes ago, and Julie had headed over to the baggage claim carousel as soon as she'd been able to ascertain which one it would be, but there was still, as of yet, no sign of her sister. She watched as other passengers collected their bags and greeted the friends and family members who had come to collect them from the airport. Surrounded by happy reunions and bags of all shapes, sizes and colours on an array of slowly spinning carousels, Julie bit her lip again, then smirked and scolded herself. *She's fine*, Julie thought firmly. *Probably just went to the washroom first, or something.* She scanned the bags still streaming past, waiting for their owners to come and liberate them from their seemingly never-ending turn on the belt. Julie checked her watch again and glanced back at the baggage carousel number, reaffirming once again that she was at the correct spot.

And that's when she saw her.

Or rather, saw *them*.

Julie's breath caught in her throat as she watched her youngest sister stroll across the floor toward her, completely engaged in smiling conversation with the blond woman next to her. Heads bent toward one another, Julie saw their hands touch briefly as they gazed at each other. It was almost intimate, really, the intensity with with they looked at one another. It was as though, to each of them, none other existed in the world. The blond whispered something into Sam's ear, and Julie smiled unconsciously as Sam threw back her head and laughed, the delightful sound of it carrying faintly across the busy airport baggage claim area. Julie had rarely heard her sister laugh with such genuine abandon, and it made her heart swell to hear it now. The blond woman with her must be a rare person indeed. Which meant, Julie knew, that this could only be Sarah.

She looked to be about the same age as Samantha, with fine blond hair pulled back in a loose ponytail, blue eyes, and a dazzling smile. She stood about an inch or so taller than Sam, but the way they walked together, moving with a fluid sort of synchronicity that couldn't be taught or learned, but that could only be a natural sense and understanding of one another, made them appear almost to be connected; joined at the hip. They moved as though they were one person instead of two. In a flash of understanding, Julie knew from that moment on, even without having spoken to either of them yet, that her little sister had truly, and finally, met her match.

As if sensing they were being watched, Sam turned her head suddenly, her blue eyes briefly searching the crowd of people milling about the area. It only took a moment or two before she spotted Julie, and her face broke into a grin as she grabbed Sarah by the hand, pulling her along behind. Julie felt her own smile match that of her sister's, and suddenly her feet were moving, each step bringing her closer to the girls now rushing headlong through the crowd toward her. They met in a crushing heap of limbs and laughter near the centre of the vast room, each talking excitedly over each other about how happy each was to see/finally meet/heard so much about one another.

After a few moments, the women reluctantly parted and stepped back a bit, each getting their first real look at the other. Julie noticed Sam was wearing her hair slightly longer than usual, and while it had grown in just as fine and soft-looking as always, she had gone from having it fairly short-cropped to letting it flop in light waves and curls around her face and down just past the nape of her neck. It was cute. Julie smiled as she took in Sam's flushed cheeks and shining eyes, realizing that this moment was perhaps the happiest she had ever seen her younger sister. She seemed somehow more comfortable in her own skin, more unafraid and unashamed than Julie had ever known her to be before. She seemed to have finally grown into herself, and Julie felt a sudden pang of pride and gratitude that she was there to bear witness to such a thing. Sam's smile faltered briefly as she looked back at Julie, then she grinned and feigned a grimace.

"Quit starin', Jules. You're making me nervous!" She turned to Sarah, jerking a thumb back over her shoulder. "I'm gonna go grab our bags, hon, okay? Stay here, keep my sister outta trouble." She smiled with a wink. "I'll be right back!" Sam started off toward the baggage carousel where their luggage was still going round and round, then paused a moment and turned back. "It's really good to see you, Jules." she said quietly. And with that, she strolled back the way she had come, already watching the bags going by to see if any looked familiar. Julie watched her go, suddenly feeling on the verge of tears. She swallowed, pushing the feeling back down inside her, and turned to smile at Sarah who, she was somewhat surprised to see, was watching her closely, a slightly

44

puzzled expression on her face.

"Are you okay?" she asked.

Julie blinked at her. The woman was astute, that was for sure. Julie doubted she let Samantha get away with much at all. She looked Sarah directly in the eye, smiled, and nodded.

"Oh yeah," she sighed, "I'm just tired today. Didn't get a lot of sleep last night, and I guess it's catching up to me now! I'll be fine in a bit." She glanced over to where Sam was standing next to the luggage carousel. She had one bag already, and had apparently spotted the other one, but rather than go over to get it, she had chosen instead to hold her jacket out over the belt, flicking it as though she were a bullfighter calling out the beast. Julie rolled her eyes.

"Your girlfriend is a dork." she said. Sarah laughed lightly, her blue eyes dancing.

"Oh no, you don't, that one's not on me! My girlfriend is wonderful. Your *sister* is a dork!"

Both women laughed then, watching as Sam collected the second bag and bowed deeply to the imagined applause of her pretend audience, apparently unaware that anyone was actually paying attention. Julie and Sarah glanced knowingly at one another, nodded, and broke into loud applause on their own, clapping their hands wildly and waving invisible kerchiefs in the air. Sam looked up, blushed a deep crimson, and took a final bow before picking up both bags and trotting over to rejoin them.

Julie reached for a bag to carry, but Sarah snatched it away from her before she could get any sort of a grip on the handle. Her self-satisfied smile disappeared just as quickly as it had come, however, when Sam reclaimed the bag and motioned at them both to lead the way. Sarah shrugged, turned to link arms with Julie, and the three made their way toward the exit, giggling like schoolgirls the entire way.

*   *   *

Sarah gazed out the window, watching the unfamiliar terrain fly by as the car she and the girls occupied sped along the highway. She felt relaxed and was enjoying herself so far, but she could sense Samantha's increasing anxiety coming from the back seat, as they grew ever closer to their destination, even without turning around to look at her. She casually reached down into the back seat and touched Sam's knee. Sam latched on immediately, seeming grateful for the contact, and Sarah gave her hand a reassuring squeeze, letting her hand linger a few moments longer to help rein Sam's growing panic back in a little bit. She turned to glance at her, alone in the back seat, after insisting that Sarah ride shotgun while Julie drove them all home. Sam's eyes were wide and her breathing seemed a little on the quick side, but upon seeing Sarah smile at her, she relaxed visibly, if not even close to completely, and Sarah turned her gaze over to Julie.

Having seen pictures of all three sisters, Julie had always felt that, while she could certainly see the family resemblance between all three, Sam and Julie really looked the most alike, to her. Sarah took in Julie's shoulder-length light brown hair, already losing its lighter summer highlights, and the same big blue eyes that all three of them shared, looking almost as huge in profile as they did when looking directly at her. Julie was roughly a head or so shorter than Sam, and Sarah knew from the photos that Emily was quite a bit taller than both of her younger siblings. She grimaced inwardly at the short-joke abuse Julie had undoubtedly had to suffer once even her baby sister had grown to be taller than she was. Julie carried herself well, though, moving with a sort of compact grace that Sam was only recently starting to acquire. Sarah noticed a sort of tired tension around Julie's eyes, however, that she'd not noticed in the pictures Sam had paraded in front of her one evening as they'd worked their way through a bottle of chardonnay. She remembered Julie's expression earlier, while she'd been watching Sam go off to collect their bags at the airport. Sarah had thought she'd seen a flicker of a deeper underlying sadness behind Julie's wistful smile, which had then been replaced immediately by the same tired tension she saw there now. Sarah wondered if Julie really was just tired, as she'd said, or if there was maybe something more to it. Sam had told her that Julie was a cancer survivor; that the disease had gone into remission years ago. *But what if...?*

Inwardly, she shook her head and silently scolded herself. Sarah had often let her imagination get the better of her, and would be leaping to conclusions and assumptions before they ever reached the house. As a child, she'd often retreated into her overactive imagination as a way of

46

keeping herself entertained. It seemed that, as an adult, old habits could still die hard. She smiled faintly, and was about to turn and look back out the window, when Julie seemed to become aware of Sarah watching her out of the corner of her eye, and turned to smile at her. Sarah returned the smile instantly. She genuinely liked Julie a lot already, and was excited to get the Meeting of Emily out of the way so that Sam would see that everything would be just fine, and so that they could all get on with enjoying the holiday weekend together. The autumn colours were out in full force, and while the temperature held a slight but crisp chill that hinted at the coming winter, the sporadic sunshine of the day indicated that summer was not entirely ready to surrender itself just yet, either.

Sarah smiled again and met Julie's quick gaze.

"So," she began, mischief dancing in her eyes, "tell me something about Sam that I wouldn't already know. Preferably something I can use for blackmail later if I have any trouble getting my own way!"

Both women in the front seat erupted in a gale of laughter as a jacket sleeve appeared suddenly from out of nowhere and swatted Sarah squarely on the back of the head. The car continued along the highway, carrying the girls ever closer to home.

*   *   *

Emily didn't so much hear the car in the driveway as she saw Trick sit bolt upright from a dead sleep on the floor in the corner of the kitchen and stare in the direction of the front hall. Anytime Emily cooked anything, Trick usually camped out nearby, particularly if the food gave off an aroma that was pleasing to his acute senses. He seemed to know, from the load of groceries that she'd returned with earlier (and was still now just finishing putting them away) that a holiday feast would soon be brewing, and apparently hadn't wanted to miss anything. The dog had grown tired of watching while she tucked all of the new food away out of sight and scent, however, and had passed out on the floor nearby, instead. Now, though, Trick sat at attention, all senses on full alert. Emily suspected that her sisters were home at last.

Emily rinsed her hands quickly at the sink, dried them on a nearby dishtowel, and took a quick appraisal of the kitchen. It wasn't exactly spotless, by any stretch, but it had a comfortable, sort of lived-in look. Samantha wouldn't mind, anyway, she was sure. She'd become so increasingly distant over the past few years in particular that Emily doubted whether Sam would notice much at all.

She heard the muffled thump of a car door being closed, and laughed as Trick fairly launched himself from the kitchen to the hallway in a single bound.

"Yes, Trick-ster, I think your girl has finally come back to see you!" Trick whined and scratched impatiently at the door, checking back over his shoulder to see how much longer Emily was going to take in getting the door open. His tail was wagging so hard, Emily wondered briefly if it might fly off one of these times.

"Easy, buddy, I'm coming!" she laughed, crossing the floor. "Here..." Emily had barely cracked the door open and Trick, nose first, had pushed his way out and was off, leaping down the steps to the driveway. Before she'd pulled the door completely open, Emily heard Trick's single ecstatic bark of greeting and Sam's squeal of laughter, cut off almost immediately when Tricky no doubt attempted to tackle her in his rush to say hello.

"Hhhiiiiii, Puppy!!!" Sam cried, in her traditional greeting for the dog, as Emily stepped onto the front porch with a smile. Samantha had always, for whatever reason, continued to refer to Trick as a puppy. Or, more specifically, as *her* puppy. Emily and Julie had tried to correct her once or twice in the beginning, but had quickly given up and let Sam have her way. After all, it didn't hurt anyone (least of all Trick who, Emily was convinced, believed that he was, in fact, still a little puppy rather than a full grown dog most of the time), and truth be told, it was rather endearing. Additionally, Emily could kind of understand the sentiment. In a lot of ways, she was fairly certain that, to her, Sam would always be her little baby sister. No matter how old she claimed to be.

And Trick, for his part, seemed to love it, really. He would get so excited he'd practically bounce straight up and down until Sam was ready to play with him, and this moment was no different. The dog was beside himself with puppy-ish glee at finally having his girl back. He loved being with Emily and Julie, of course, but there'd never been any doubt in anyone's mind that Trick and Sam belonged together. Emily had often thought she'd almost be jealous of their instant bond - were it not so adorable to watch, that is.

Her smile widened as she watched Trick bounce between Sam and Julie, now both standing next to the car. To him, both women had been gone close to forever, even though he'd seen Julie just hours before. As far as Trick was concerned, they'd both been gone, and they'd both come back, and now they were all together again at long last. It was hard not to get caught up in that kind of excitement, Emily decided. Besides, he was right. They were, in fact, all together again at last.

Just then, the passenger side door opened and a third person stepped out. A woman Emily had never seen before, with blond hair pulled back in a ponytail and bright blue eyes, their colour highlighted all the more by the sweater she'd just finished pulling over her head to beat back the slight chill of the autumn air. She was smiling warmly at Sam and Julie, chuckling at Trick, who had only just now noticed her and went to give her a similar greeting as he'd just given the girls. She bent over and scratched his ears while his lightning-fast tongue attempted to slather her face with well-intentioned doggie kisses. The woman laughed, kissing the top of his head, before sending him back to bounce between Sam and Julie once again.

Then, calmly and self-assuredly, the woman turned her eyes on Emily, gazing at her intently for a moment, before her face broke into an easy and disarming smile. She glanced over to Sam, who hadn't yet noticed her sister standing on the porch beyond the still-bouncing dog, then looked at Emily again, and started walking purposefully in her direction. Emily found that she couldn't look away from the warmth in the woman's seemingly genuine smile, but out of the corner of her eye, she saw Sam's head suddenly shoot up as she finally noticed Emily standing there, and realized that the blond woman with them was now mounting the stairs to the porch where Emily waited, wrapping her arms tightly around herself for a moment to help keep warm. The woman, now at the top of the stairs, smiled again and extended her hand in introduction.

"Hi there, you must be Emily. I'm Sarah." The two women shook hands as Samantha and Julie moved to join them, Sam seeming to rush a

49

little more than did her sister. "I'm very happy to meet you," Sarah continued. "I've heard so much about you!"

Emily nodded, a little confused, and looked at Sam and Julie to see if they could fill in some of the missing pieces for her. Julie stepped up and, seeing her shiver, wrapped an arm around Emily's shoulders in a sort of half hug.

"Sarah is going to be joining us for the weekend," Julie explained. "She's Sam's..."

"Friend from school." Sam cut in quickly. "She...um...didn't have anywhere to go for the holiday. So I offered to let her come here and spend it with us, instead." She glanced at Julie, her gaze then quickly ducking to the ground. Then she looked back at Emily. "If, that is, it's okay with you? I was going to call, but it all happened so last minute..." her voice trailed off.

Emily looked from one woman to the other, still confused. Something was wrong, but she couldn't quite tell what it was. Whoever Sarah was, though, it seemed she was important to Sam, judging from the pleading look on her face just now, when she'd just asked if Sarah could stay with them for the weekend. Emily decided the details could wait. For now, she just wanted to hug her sister, welcome her home, and somehow get the smile Emily had just seen back onto Sam's face again. Her smile came so rarely, that Emily wanted to hang onto it for as long and as often as possible.

"Of course, we have plenty of room," she smiled, noticing Sam's shoulders relax somewhat. "Sarah," Emily turned to face her, "you are welcome here, anytime. Our home is your home." Sarah returned the smile and thanked her, then bent to pick up one of the bags they'd brought. Emily picked up another bag, which Julie promptly took from her, and turned to open the front door.

"Let's get in out of the cold now, shall we?" she asked, holding the door open for them all. Trick was the first one in, followed by Julie and Sarah. Suddenly, Emily felt Sam's arms close around her waist in a tight bear hug. Still holding the door with one hand, she let the other fall to rest on Sam's hands, giving her a gentle squeeze.

"It's good to see you, Em," Sam whispered softly into her ear. Emily swallowed past the sudden painful lump rising in her throat.

"You too," she responded quietly. "Welcome home, baby sister."

With that, Sam released her just as suddenly and disappeared into the house. Emily followed, closing the door behind her, and rested back against it for a moment to catch her breath. Something was definitely going on with her youngest sibling and, while Emily wasn't sure what it could be, she knew from the look on Sam's face moments ago that she would be best off not to push anything just yet. For now, her sisters were both home, safe and getting warmed up, all together under one roof.

That's enough, Emily thought to herself as she made her way back to the kitchen, listening to the happy chatter the other women were engaging in while putting the bags away and hanging jackets in the front hallway. *Having her here, safe and sound, is enough for me to know.*

Emily sighed quietly as she crossed the kitchen and finished putting the groceries away. She tilted her head in response to the laughter already coming from the other room. *At least,* she decided, *it's enough for me to know...for now.* At that, Emily left the room and headed off into the house to join the others. It was already turning out to be a very interesting weekend, indeed.

~5~

Sam paced the room, her room, nervously, while Sarah examined every photo and knick-knack in view. She was beginning to realize how much 'stuff' she really had, though she'd never thought much about it before. She'd always felt safest and most comfortable if she surrounded herself with things she loved, things that meant something to her, and things that reminded her of happier times. Over the years, she now realized, she had amassed a LOT of things. And Sarah was now standing in the middle of it all, inspecting it all, asking questions and listening to her stories with that same quiet, thoughtful smile on her face the whole time. It seemed they'd been in there for hours, though Sam knew it had really only been about twenty minutes, or so. Still, they were taking too long. Trick had already grown tired and was curled up on the end of her bed, snoring lightly.

"We should go out and join the others," she said, trying to sound casual. "They're likely to wonder what we're up to in here." Sam grimaced inwardly at her feeble attempt at a joke. Sarah straightened from looking at something scribbled on an old sheet of paper on Sam's desk, and turned to look at her curiously.

"What could we possibly be up to in here?" Sarah asked, eyes wide open in mock innocence. "What with me just being your homeless school *friend*, and all..."

Sam groaned and covered her face with one hand. She'd known it. As soon as the words were out of her mouth, she'd wanted to take them back, but she'd felt like suddenly she was on some sort of rollercoaster. And now it had just gone off the tracks and out of control.

"Sare..." she began apologetically, but Sarah held up a hand to cut her off.

"Don't," she said. "I get it, I do." She took a deep breath, as though she were reluctant to continue. But continue she did, anyway. "I just really think you need to stop hiding so much, and let your sisters know you more for who you really are. It's not so terrible, the person you are, you know. No one is going to stop loving you because of it. In fact, they may just love you more, if you let them." She crossed the room and gently tugged Sam's hand down away from her face so she could gaze directly into her eyes, making sure she again had her full attention. A tear slipped down Sam's cheek, and Sarah wiped it away softly with her thumb before she continued.

"Besides," she whispered, "what makes you think Emily doesn't already know?" Sam's eyes grew wide and she shook her head.

"Jules would never..."

"No," Sarah interrupted before Sam could fly off on her, "not Jules. Of course not. But you're the one who keeps telling me how brilliant Emily is; how so much smarter than you she is. So what makes you think she couldn't have possibly figured all of this out for herself? Maybe even long ago?" Sarah smiled, bemused at the skeptical look on Sam's face. "Don't take this the wrong way, hon," she smiled, "but you're not exactly the straightest-looking person I've ever met. NOT that that's a bad thing! It's just...I think it's maybe more obvious than you think. And not as big a deal, either, by the way, but you'll have to figure that one out for yourself, really. I'm just sayin'...it's very possible that she already knows. Either way, you trying to hide it isn't doing either of you any good. Hiding something doesn't make it not true, and only really means that you are continuing to lie about who you really are to your sister, who pretty much raised you, and who probably deserves to be treated better than that, as a result."

Sam felt herself crumbling and breaking down again, and tried to pull away, but Sarah refused to let her go. Instead, she pulled Sam into a tight hug, stroking her hair as she spoke quietly into the silence of the room.

"Sweetheart, I love you more than my luggage, but you have to get this out. It's eating you up inside, and it's killing me to watch. Let's just tell her and get it out in the open where it can all be dealt with. I'll be

53

right there with you, and honestly, I'm willing to bet that she already figured it out long ago."

Sam pulled back enough to look at her girlfriend, tears now flowing freely and unchecked down her face.

"You really think so? That Emily could already know about me?" she sniffled. Sarah smiled, then chuckled softly.

"I knew the moment I first saw you," she grinned. "In fact, I believe that my first thought upon meeting you was something along the lines of, '*Gay. Cute. Mine.*' It was something like that..." she nodded, feigning seriousness. Sam sniffed again, then smiled wanly.

"That's..." she chuckled, then began to giggle in earnest. "That's ridiculous. You..." Unable to contain herself any longer, Sam doubled over and laughed, trying vainly to wipe her tears away with the back of her hand. "I need a Kleenex, or something..." she said, still laughing, as she looked around the room.

"Sweetie, you need a whole *BOX*!" Sarah teased, reaching to grab one from Sam's desk. "Here." Sarah tossed the Kleenex box over to where Sam stood, leaning against the wall, still laughing and trying to catch her breath. She caught it easily and dissolved into a fit of giggles again.

"A whole *box*?! Really?!"

Sarah nodded, watching as Samantha mopped herself up with the tissue she'd provided.

"Yes. In fact, from the looks of things, I may have to run out and get you some more..."

Sam smirked at her.

"Okay, that's enough. You can stop now."

"Mayhaps if I were to just hose you down completely, we could just start all over..." Sarah cut off, squealing as Sam closed the space between them so quickly she'd barely had time to blink. Before she could catch her breath, Sam had wrapped her arms around her and pulled her into a tight hug, kissing her softly on the lips as she did so. Sarah's eyes closed as she melted into the moment, and Sam smiled, reluctant to pull away again.

"OK," she whispered, kissing Sarah's forehead, then the tip of her nose. "Let's go get this over with before I lose whatever's left of my nerve." She grabbed Sarah's hand and together they crossed the room to the door. Sam sighed as she reached for the doorknob and turned it, pulling the door open and stepping through into the hallway. "I need a drink."

Sarah smiled and kissed the back of Sam's neck.

"Soon, lovely," she promised quietly. "I'll even get it for you. We just have to do one little thing first, if you're ready."

Sam sighed again as they headed down the hall, Trick padding happily along behind, not letting the girls out of his sight.

"Ready as I'll ever be, I guess," she muttered, jaw tightening. Her stomach dropped as she led the way down the stairs to the kitchen, where she could hear Jules and Em talking as they prepared dinner. *What the hell am I going to say?* Sam wondered. *I have no idea how to do this.*

She *should* have had some idea, she realized, but it had been so easy with Jules. Julie had just asked her one day. All Sam had had to do was answer truthfully. That had been hard enough, but ultimately okay. Sam had the sudden realization that she'd never actually started a conversation about her sexuality before. She'd always depended on others to start it for her, or for it to just be an unspoken understanding. She'd never had to sit someone down and say the words. She supposed she always *had* been hiding, just like Sarah had said.

And now, she was going to try actually 'coming out', for the first time. With Emily, of all people. Sam groaned inwardly. She felt sick.

Sam paused for a fleeting moment before rounding the corner into the kitchen, but felt Sarah's reassuring squeeze on her hand and gentle nudge from behind. They stepped together into the room, and Sam watched as both of her sisters straightened up from whatever private conversation they'd just been having, and turned to look at them. Julie smiled, and Sam noticed Emily's glance to Sarah, still holding Sam's hand,

55

then her smile as she looked back at Sam.

"A-ha!" she exclaimed, "There you are! We were wondering where you two had disappeared to!" Sam felt herself go pale as her breath caught in her throat. Sarah gave her hand another squeeze, then let go, moving around her to go stand between Sam and Julie.

"Well, something sure smells delicious, Emily!" Sarah said with enthusiasm, smiling that grin that always made Sam's knees go weak. Trouble was, her knees already felt like they were about to give out, but for an entirely different reason. Swallowing, Sam forced her feet to move forward, as well.

"Yeah," she agreed. "What's for dinner, Em?"

Emily looked from Sam to Sarah and back again, still smiling. Then her smile faded, her expression turning instead to one of dismay.

"Oh...it's..." she stammered. Sam had never seen her sister at such a loss for words, and puzzled at what the problem was, now. Emily sighed and started again.

"We made lasagna, Jules and I..." she said, gesturing vaguely in Julie's direction. "I'm so sorry, I didn't even think to ask, Sarah..." Emily turned, flustered, and looked at Sarah directly. "I wasn't thinking. It's a meat lasagna, and I didn't even think...I should have asked, if you have any...dietary...restrictions, or...?" Sam gaped at her sister. *What the hell is wrong with her all of a sudden*, she wondered. *What's she doing?*

Before Sam could interject, Sarah calmly stepped over to the counter, reaching across and taking Emily's hand.

"I'm sure it tastes every bit as wonderful as it smells, and I can not wait," she replied smoothly, seeming to diffuse Emily's sudden case of nerves as easily as she did so often with Samantha's. She grinned up at Emily again, ticking points off on her fingers as she made them. "I love meat - *total* carnivore - I am not a huge fan of seafood but have been known to ingest it in small portions from time to time, I have no known allergies, food or otherwise, and I have a distinct weakness for anything involving chocolate," she finished with a wink. "It's like my Kryptonite."

Emily and Julie both burst into laughter, Emily squeezing Sarah's hand in appreciation.

"Well, then, I imagine you'll fit right in here!" she chuckled. Julie threw one arm casually around Sarah's shoulders.

"I think maybe she does already, really!" she smiled. Sarah laughed lightly.

"I do try." she grinned.

"You don't have to try," Emily protested, shaking her head. "It's done. You are one of us...another member of the Collins Sisterhood. One can never have too many younger sisters, right Jules? I mean, for the longest time, Julie was carrying the torch all by herself, but was finally able to pass it on to Sam..." Emily glanced over at Samantha, still frozen on the sidelines, unable to believe her ears. She was torn between not wanting to interrupt the banter that was going on between her sisters and her girlfriend, but suddenly concerned as to the direction in which it was heading. Em smiled at her again before turning her attention back to Sarah. Sam thought she saw Emily wink playfully at Jules, and she felt her stomach drop. The rollercoaster was careening off the tracks again.

"For my part, I was always happy to have another little sister," Emily continued good-naturedly, "but I often wondered if our parents hadn't had other ideas." Sam visibly blanched as Emily went on, not noticing her youngest sister's sudden and extreme discomfort. "I mean, really, they waited so many years to have another kid, and then when they finally do, it's yet another girl. *And* they name her '*Sam*'?!" Emily laughed, engaged in her own personal recollections, and seemingly unaware that the room had just grown silent. Samantha stared in abject terror, mouth hanging open, wanting everything to stop but unable to make a sound. She barely heard Emily's next words as she turned and bolted from the room.

"They may have thought they'd wanted a boy, but I always knew our Samie-Sam was meant to be a girl. And as it turned out, none of us could have asked for...more..." Her voice trailed off as she watched Trick leap to his feet and chase after Samantha. Emily stared at the empty kitchen doorway through which her sister had just disappeared, then

57

jumped as she heard the front door slam closed.

"Oh God..." Julie whispered into the silent room.

"I'll get her," Sarah stated decisively, turning to follow after Sam.

"No," Emily said, quietly, but firmly. "No, I'll go." Her eyes moved from Sarah to Julie, silently pleading for their understanding. "I...um...I think I need to, this time. I think it needs to be me." Her words hung in the air a moment as the two women considered. Then Sarah gave a curt nod and, to Emily's surprise and relief, rounded the counter between them and gave Emily a quick hug.

"Go get our girl," Sarah whispered, "and bring her back home."

Emily nodded quietly as she blinked back tears. She grabbed her jacket from the hallway where Trick waited to get out, having been a moment too late to join his Samantha when she left. Emily absently scratched his head, thinking to herself for a moment. Then, almost as an after-thought, she picked up an umbrella, as well as Sam's jacket, which had been left forgotten on its hook in her head-long rush to get out of the house.

Emily opened the front door, holding Trick by his collar, and looked outside. The sunshine had left, hidden now behind darkening grey clouds. The air felt as though rain, snow, or perhaps both, were imminent. Sam was nowhere in sight, but Emily wasn't too concerned. If she knew her sister at all, she had a fairly good idea as to where she might be. Checking the sky once again, she pulled her jacket on, instructed Trick to stay put, and stepped out into the growing gloom, closing the door behind her.

*   *   *

Sam stood at the river's edge, shivering in the cold, first drops of rain. She wished she had thought to grab her jacket before she left, but she hadn't been thinking of much at the time. Only that she'd needed to get away. She had arrived at the shore of the river a few minutes before, but was still breathing heavily, her cheeks flushed, tears streaming down her face. The cold water babbled along past her, indifferent to her current state of mind. Yet something about it brought her a hint of the peace she'd been looking for when her feet had carried her there.

Her sisters had taken her to that spot when she was very young; one of the first times she could remember having been invited to play with them. They'd spent a few summers all together there, climbing trees and building forts in amongst the bushes lining the shore. It had become their secret spot and, even after the other two had found other things to do with their time, Sam had continued to make it hers. She'd spent hours alone, listening to the water flow past her as she stretched out in the soft grass below the overhanging branches of the great willow tree, reading quietly to herself and, later on, writing parts of stories and poems that came to her when she was feeling somewhat creative.

This was where she had come the night her parents had been killed, arriving at the river's edge in a similar state to the one in which she now found herself. That time, she'd thrown herself to the frozen ground and wailed into the night, certain that her young life was over. In some ways, she supposed now, it had been.

The wind started picking up as Sam paced back and forth along the river, hands in fists at her side. Her breath heaved in sobbing gasps as the first drops of rain began to fall. She didn't know what to do; how to feel. She wished Sarah were there to help calm her the way only she could, but Sam had left her behind in her sudden unexpected anguish. Even poor Trick hadn't been able to follow along this time. Sam clapped both fists to the sides of her head, beating on herself in frustration. She'd done that a lot after her parents had been killed...her despair had often become so overwhelming that she'd found small ways to hurt herself physically, feeling that it was the only way she could release the build-up of pressure inside. She hadn't done anything even remotely like that in probably 20 years, but now she found herself feeling like very much the broken 7-year-old girl she'd once been. The emotional turmoil of that horrible night so long ago had all come crashing back on her with Em's simple comment about their parents wanting a boy. It was a joke that had been made a thousand times before...Samantha herself had even run with it more than once...but on this night, for some reason, it had set her off and sent her flying from the house in anguish yet again.

Not for some reason, Sam thought, still sobbing. "You know the reason," she muttered aloud to herself. "You know...they don't know, but you know. The reason..." she choked as another sob wrenched her body, the rain coming down much harder now. Samantha closed her eyes against the onslaught of wind and rain as her mind flashed back to that one terrible night, and the moment that had changed her life forever.

She and Julie, done with trick-or-treating for another year, had lugged their sugar-filled haul back toward the house. It wasn't until they'd rounded the corner that they'd noticed the lights from the police car, and the small crowd gathering in front of their home; an eclectic array of ghosts and goblins mixed with pajama-clad young children held in their parents' arms. Sam hadn't understood what was happening, at first. She'd become alarmed, though, when Julie had grabbed hold of her hand and run, causing Sam to drop her hard-earned candy on the sidewalk and leave it behind as she was dragged the remaining distance to their front porch.

Two police officers were there, a young man not much older than Emily, and a woman, who looked to be about the same age. They were talking to Emily, and Em was in tears. A woman who'd lived next door was standing there in the doorway, as well, her arm around Emily, consoling her. When Em had spotted her sisters running up the driveway toward her, she'd broken free of all three of them and rushed down the steps to meet them. She'd flung her arms around both girls and sobbed. Sam hadn't been able to make out much of what she was saying, but it was enough to frighten her, and set her to crying, as well. Julie had stood in mute shock for a few moments, and then had helped to usher her sisters back toward the warmth of the house, where the two officers waited respectfully.

Taking Sam's tear-stained face in her hands, Jules had whispered the horrible truth to her that night, as though saying it quietly could somehow make it less true. Mom and Dad were dead, and would not be coming home to them ever again.

The rest of the evening wasn't much more than a blur to Sam. She'd cried continually but quietly as Emily and Julie had spoken with the police officers. The officers had both been very kind; the man's gentle brown eyes, in particular, had been somber, almost as though he was somehow sharing in their loss. It was the woman who, in trying to help the girls understand the atrocity that had befallen them all that night, had spoken the words that had become forever burned into Samantha's young mind.

"There's no reason for what happened," she had said. "They were just in the wrong place at the wrong time."

The wrong time. Sam had heard the words echo over and over in her head. *Wrong time.*

Unable to thwart or contain the swell of terrible understanding that had washed over her in that moment, Sam had suddenly leapt up from the couch and bolted from the house, letting her feet carry her, without thinking, to the bank of the river; the only place, other than home, where she'd felt safe, protected and happy. From that night on, however, she knew she'd never deserve to feel any of those things again. *The wrong time.*

Now, so many years later, she again found herself at the bank of that same river, in that same spot, feeling just as overwhelmed with despair as she had been that night. Wind whipping her soaking wet hair, Sam spun on the river, as though it had just said something to anger her.

"The reason?!" she screamed at it. "You *know* the reason! You know...the reason...is *you!* You're...the...*you're* the reason..." With a cry, Samantha clapped her fists to her head again, doubling over as sobs wracked her body once again.

"Sam." The voice came to her so quietly, Sam almost didn't hear it over the gales of wind whipping about her. She froze, listening. She didn't need to turn around to know who was standing there. She was, after all, the one who had first found Sam there that awful Halloween night, as well. The night she'd thought her life had ended. Her body sagging in defeat, Sam turned slowly, eyes gazing steadily at the ground, afraid to look up. She swallowed self-consciously and licked her lips, tasting at once the salt from her tears mixed with the drops of rain that were cascading down her face. She couldn't seem to summon her voice, but even if she could, she didn't know what she should say.

She glanced up, cautiously, and saw her standing there a few feet away, keeping her distance and yet remaining close enough that they didn't have to shout over the rain. She was somewhat damp, herself; her

61

short, light brown hair clinging in patches to her scalp, while other parts had already begun to stick out at odd angles. Sam might have laughed at the image if she hadn't felt so miserable. And if it had been anyone other than Emily.

She had, however, managed to remain mostly dry, having thought to bring an umbrella with her when she'd left the house to fetch her wayward sister. *Always prepared,* Sam thought. She'd have made a good boy scout. She'd even managed to bring Sam's jacket, she saw. Not that it would do her much good now, drenched as she was already, but it might help stop her shivering so much. Em always seemed to get everything right, Sam realized with a distraught sigh. *And I...I do not.* She glanced back at the ground, not trusting herself to speak.

"Sam," Emily said again, just as quietly, as she extended her arm and offered Sam her jacket, "come back to the house. Please." Sam shook her head.

"Can't," she muttered hopelessly. The wind had started to quiet, but the rain continued to pour down on both of them. Emily almost seemed to be encased in a bubble of mostly-dry under her umbrella. It looked warm and comforting to Sam, but she remained where she was, unable to move, and feeling like she didn't belong there, anyway. Emily ducked her head, trying to get a better look at her sister's face. Sam stood frozen to her spot, fists at her sides, head down, shivering so hard that Emily thought she may actually be starting to turn blue.

"Why can't you, Samie," she asked gently. "You're cold, you're soaking wet, you're..."

"I'm gay." There. She'd said it. Sam held her breath, praying for Emily to break the silence somehow. Her prayer was answered a few awkward moments later, just not in the way she'd expected.

"What?" Emily asked. Sam sighed, and struggled to find the strength to say it again. She was getting so tired.

"I'm...Sarah's...my girlfriend. Not just my friend from school. She's...I love her. And she loves me, too...I think..." Sam choked off another sob, took a shaky breath, and tried to continue, but Emily cut her off.

"Anyone can see that, Samie," she said. "I'm so glad that you finally told me yourself, and I am so very proud of you for having the courage to bring Sarah here so we could meet her. I like her a lot already. She seems like an incredible woman...and a pretty perfect match for you, if you ask me."

Sam stared at the ground, unsure about what she was feeling. She was afraid to look at Emily again, lest she saw laughter behind her eyes, making everything she'd just said turn out to be some kind of colossal joke.

It hadn't sounded like a joke, though. Not even a little bit.

Sam raised her head and met her sister's calm blue eyes. Instead of laughter, the love that she saw reflecting back at her nearly weakened her knees, and she began to cry again, softly this time. The rain was turning more to a light drizzle, but neither woman noticed. Instead they continued to stand stone still, each watching the other, truly seeing one another for the first time. Sam was first to break the silence.

"You knew?" she asked. Emily nodded slowly.

"I didn't know how to bring it up, or if I even should. So I never said anything." She shrugged. "To be honest, I never really felt the need. It just always seemed to be so natural for you. Just another part of who you are." She took a step closer and stopped again. Sam held her ground. "It was always just one more thing to love about you, Sam."

Sam didn't know what to say. This was not going at all the way that she'd planned. Emily was watching her, a curious look on her face. Samantha began fidgeting self-consciously with the cuffs of her wet sleeves. Emily held Sam's jacket out again, this time gesturing Sam to come closer so that Emily could wrap it around her shoulders. Sam wiped a hand absently across her eyes and, sniffling quietly, took a shaky step forward. Emily moved toward her and wrapped the damp jacket around Sam's shaking form, pulling her into a warm embrace under her umbrella as she did so. She could feel Sam shivering in her arms, and she rubbed her back rapidly, hoping the friction would help to start warming her up again.

"I didn't realize how hard this would be for you, Samie," she whispered. "I would have said something long ago if I'd thought it would have helped you in some way." She paused, listening to Sam's breathing against her shoulder as she struggled to regain control, her face buried in the front of Emily's coat. "I don't think any of that is the reason that you came running out here tonight, though" she said quietly, pausing again when she felt Samantha stiffen even further in her arms. "But I don't need to know the reason. Not right now." Sam relaxed somewhat, and lifted her head to look up at her sister.

"You can always tell me if you want to, though, okay?" she said, wiping the remaining drops of rain from the girl's face. It was at times like this that Sam seemed so much younger to Emily. *Probably because she still looks the same as she did when she was seventeen,* Emily thought absently. She pushed Sam's soaking wet hair out of her eyes. "I want you to know that. You can tell me anything, any time. Okay?"

At Sam's slow nod, Emily smiled gently down at her.

"I love you, so much, baby sister. You know that?" Sam's lip quivered, threatening to release another torrent of tears, but she managed to quell it for the time being. Sam nodded again.

"I love you, too, Em," she said in a low voice. "And...I'm sorry..."

Emily shushed her with a quick kiss to her forehead, and smiled again.

"No sorries. But we have to get you back inside." Her voice lowered conspiratorially. "For one thing, Trick is mightily peeved at being left behind by BOTH of us." Emily grinned, steering Sam back toward the house, but keeping her arm around her as they walked. "And for another thing...we've totally left your girlfriend alone at the house...with Jules."

Sam stopped and stared at her sister in mock horror.

"Oh no..."

"Oh yes," Emily laughed. "I think they were about the break out some old photo albums when I left." The women started walking again, a little faster this time. "I wonder which pictures of you Jules will show off first? The Baby Bare Butt shots or the Baby Bath Time Bubbles series?"

Giggling, Sam broke into a run, but stopped and turned back after only a few steps, her expression again serious.

"Thanks, Em," she said sincerely. "Thanks for coming to get me...and...everything..."

Emily put her arm around Sam's waist and the two began walking again.

"Any time, kiddo," Emily said, equally sincere. "Any time, and every time."

Sam nodded again, though she knew that she could never tell Em the truth of what she knew, of what she'd learned that night long ago. If anyone ever found out...Sam knew without a doubt that her sisters would never forgive her. She would lose Sarah, and she would be completely alone, and unloved, for the rest of her days.

And she would deserve it.

No, Sam decided firmly to herself. *No one can ever know.*

A more comfortable silence fell over the pair as they walked back home together. The rain had stopped completely by the time they reached the front porch. It seemed as though, for now at least, the storm had finally abated.

But Samantha knew better. The turmoil inside of her, that had set her off and running tonight, was not gone. It would always be with her, as it had been ever since that night; the night she'd discovered the awful secret which she still now carried with her each and every day. The secret no one knew but her, and that no one could ever know.

There's no reason for what happened, the police officer lady had said. *They were just in the wrong place at the wrong time.*

But there *was* a reason, Sam knew. The terrible understanding - the truth - that had come over her that night was that s*he* was the reason. Samantha had known, in that moment,and in every moment since, that her parents' death had been entirely her fault.

65

~6~

Sarah lay awake, curled on her side in bed, listening to Sam's quiet breathing next to her. Trick lay sprawled across the foot of the bed, his head on Sam's leg, snoring contentedly. Despite how smoothly the remainder of their evening had appeared to go, it had taken some firm persuasion, and quite a bit of rum, to get Sam to sleep. Now that she was finally resting, Sarah kissed her shoulder and, being careful not to wake her, rolled silently onto her back, her mind going over all that had happened throughout the day.

All Sarah really knew about what happened between Emily and Sam when they'd been out in the rain was that Sam had finally told Em about her and Sarah. Emily had, of course, been magnificent about it, and had welcomed Sarah into the family with arms even more wide open than they had been before. Sam had been soaked and smiling, but Sarah had noticed a sort of covert abject fear in her eyes, behind the smile and ever-present humour that Sam routinely put forward. She'd noticed it before, many times, but this was the most pronounced that Sarah had ever seen it. And it frightened her.

For the first time since Sarah had known her, Samantha seemed about ready to break.

The girls had ushered her into a hot shower almost immediately, while Sarah helped the sisters finish preparing dinner. Sam had joined them later; hair wet, skin still pink and warm from the heat of the water. She'd pulled on an old, faded and over-sized sweatshirt and loose flannel pants, looking for all the world like a fresh-faced college student, rather than a 32-year-old woman. She'd seemed more relaxed and comfortable, to be sure, but Sarah could still sense the tension in her, and wondered if she had, in fact, gotten everything she'd needed to out in the open with

Emily, or if there were somehow more to it all.

The rest of the evening had been splendid, however, and Sarah found herself really beginning to love these girls, already. They'd split two bottles of chardonnay between the three of them, while Samantha had casually made her way through about a third of the once-full bottle of rum that her sisters had happened to have on hand. They had laughed through dinner, eyes twinkling in the candlelight as they'd each told stories of what life had been like growing up together.

Sarah had been fascinated. She had always wanted a sister, but had been...'blessed', was the supposed word for it...with a younger brother, instead. They were closer in age than were the Collins siblings, and had spent their childhood fighting and playing together in a small town to the north. Their parents were still happily married, and Sarah and her brother both returned home regularly to visit and enjoy more of their mother's home-cooked meals. Sarah's life could not have been much different from Sam's, she'd realized. As such, she had spent the rest of the evening with a permanent grin on her face, listening as the three sisters teased and provoked one another good-naturedly, while Trick had fallen asleep in front of the crackling fireplace.

Sarah had been delighted and somewhat surprised to find that the women were all equally fascinated and interested in her life, as well - where she had come from, what her dreams had been, where she'd wanted her life to take her next. They'd asked about life in a small town, versus theirs of growing up in a city. And they'd demanded every gruesome detail of the "gross boy stuff" that she could remember from her brother's antics as a young child.

They'd told stories and laughed long into the night, until the wine was gone and they were wiping tears from their eyes. Sam was curled on the couch next to her, fingers entwined with Sarah's, as they'd each helped recount for Emily the tale of how they'd met while standing in line waiting to register for a week-long writer's workshop, and the subsequent path their growing love and affection for one another had taken them. For all of Sam's worrying, the creative writing issue was a non-issue where Emily was concerned. She'd beamed proudly at her youngest sister, momentarily at a loss for words, before quietly asking if she could read some of what Samantha had written someday. Sam had simply nodded, also unable to speak, and had laid her head down on Sarah's shoulder for a time.

After a while, Sarah noticed Sam's eyes drooping, and had caught Julie's eye. Taking her cue, Julie stretched and yawned, saying that it had been a very long day for all of them, and that she'd needed to 'hit the hay', as she'd put it. Emily quickly agreed, and the women had all hugged and kissed one another before heading upstairs to their rooms. Samantha had curled up in Sarah's arms and was asleep even before her head hit the pillow.

While Sarah lay there, turning all of the day's events over in her mind, Sam suddenly stiffened next to her, and let out a small, whimpering cry. Sarah rolled over, wrapping both arms around Samantha's shaking form, and whispered gentle, soothing words into her ear. After a few moments, Sam's body relaxed, and her breathing evened out, becoming regular again. Sarah smoothed down her hair, kissed the back of her head, and closed her eyes, gradually drifting off into a dreamless sleep.

*   *   *

Julie awoke with a start, gasping in pain. Sitting up, she pressed one hand to her abdomen, trying in vain to ease the sudden agony that had gripped her from within, and woke her from a dead sleep. She sat still for a moment, trying to catch her breath, but when the pain grew worse, she rolled out of bed and, nearly doubled-over, and made her way, as quietly as she could, down the carpeted hallway to the washroom. She waited until she had closed and locked the door behind her before flipping on the light. One hand gripping the counter's edge, and the other still pressed to her stomach, Julie stared at her reflection in the mirror. Sweat-soaked hair framed her pale face, dark circles under her eyes standing in stark contrast to the sudden whiteness of her skin. Julie took a few quick, shallow breaths, struggling to regain control of her raging insides. She turned on the cold water tap, and splashed a handful of the refreshing liquid onto her face, then gazed once again at her dripping reflection, breathing hard. Feeling the bile rise in her throat, she spun and vomited into the nearby toilet, hoping in the back of her mind that the running water would drown out any other sound.

The pain eased somewhat as she flushed and, using the countertop as leverage, Julie pulled herself back to a standing position. She splashed more cool water onto her face, and turned off the tap. She would have to tell them, she knew. She couldn't hide this forever.

Just not now, she prayed. *Not this weekend. Please just let us have this weekend.*

Patting her face dry with a hand towel, Julie reached to flick off the light again before opening the door and stepping into the hallway. The house was still dark and quiet, though she could tell that the dawn was not far off. Julie made her way back down the hall to her bedroom, and quietly clicked the door closed behind her. Exhausted, she tumbled into bed and instantly fell back asleep.

Unbeknownst to Julie, however, another door down the hall had opened when she'd entered the washroom, and a dark form had silently kept watch from within until Julie had made her way back to her room.

Knowing that Julie was alright, for now at least, Sarah quietly closed Sam's door again, and returned to bed, deeply troubled by what she had just seen.

*   *   *

Emily managed to get up before everyone else, despite their late night, but it still wasn't as early as she'd intended. She didn't really care this time, though. The fun and mostly relaxed atmosphere of the previous evening had been more than worth it, as had the incident with Samantha by the river. Emily knew, without a doubt, that something far deeper than Sam had admitted so far was still troubling her youngest sibling, but she had seemed so...fragile...so close to her breaking point, that Emily had decided to let it go for the time being. She felt that she and Sam had taken a step closer to one another last night...a very big step, in fact...and Emily had no intention of ruining that by pushing too hard and too soon for more than Sam was ready to give.

For reasons Emily could never fathom, Samantha had always seemed at once reverent of her eldest sibling, and more than a little frightened of her, as well. Sam and Julie had always had a natural affinity for one another, while Jules and Emily had always been the best of friends. For some reason, though, Emily had never been able to get past whatever invisible hurdles had erected themselves between herself and Sam. There had always been a kind of awkward gap there...a certain distance...between them. When she was younger, Emily had often felt pangs of jealousy when watching the ease with which Jules and Sam related to one another. They had a level of friendship and trust that even surpassed the closeness that any of the girls had shared with their parents. And they still did, to this day. If possible, it had actually grown stronger over the years, as both women had blossomed into and through their adult years. Emily would never begrudge either of her sisters that kind of closeness, of course. There were times, though, when it hurt her to not be a part of it.

Emily hauled the turkey out of the small cube freezer they kept in the pantry, preferring to use it when possible over the larger deep freezer kept out in the garage. It was a heavy bird, to be sure, and Emily was glad that she'd opted to go bigger than usual this year, intending to send some leftovers back to school with Sam. With the addition of Sarah, however, it was big still enough to feed the four of them, and have some leftover, as well. Thinking of Sarah, Emily smiled to herself. She found she already loved the woman, and was so overjoyed to see how happy she made Sam. The two girls had a kind of innate chemistry, and often seemed to be speaking a secret language all their own. Emily had never seen Samantha so relaxed with another person before and, while she supposed that just having it all out in the open and not having to hide her feelings anymore may have helped with her comfort level, she sensed that there was much more to it than that. The two women just seemed to belong together. They completed each other. It was so wonderful to witness that Emily's heart swelled just thinking about it, and she smiled again. For some reason, Officer Ryan Mullen's face popped into her mind, seemingly out of nowhere, and Emily immediately, if somewhat regretfully, thrust it aside. She was never going to see him again, anyway, so there was no sense in dwelling on it anymore. She staggered across the kitchen, cradling the holiday beast in her arms, and flung it unceremoniously into the sink at the first opportunity. She cringed at the level of noise it had made, and hoped that she hadn't just woken the house up before she'd really even gotten started on her day.

Rolling up her sleeves, Emily set to thawing the turkey, then washed her hands in the adjacent sink and toweled off, mentally checking her 'to do' list for the day. She wanted to get as much done in the morning as she could, so that there would be less to do after they'd all returned from their traditional annual family pumpkin farm excursion. Every year, while they were all together for Thanksgiving, they would go to a nearby pumpkin farm and each sister would choose the pumpkin which they would then later carve for Halloween. Their parents had taken them every year and, while they were there, their mother had always used the opportunity to pick up other seasonal fruits, jams, spices and the like, as well. Their parents had loved Thanksgiving, but Halloween was always the favourite family holiday, and the pumpkin shopping trip was of utmost importance to all. After their parents had died, the girls had decided to keep the tradition, but young Samantha then had an idea that first year which would alter it and make it their own. In addition, they hoped, it would also help to make their parents' absence this time of year, in particular, hurt just a little bit less.

Emily pulled various ingredients from the refrigerator and cupboards, and began tearing up a loaf of bread to be used in her stuffing. She shook her head, smiling wanly. She never would have imagined, back in high school, that this would be her life. Emily had graduated at the top of her class, and was named Valedictorian of her senior year. She was well-liked, a decent athlete who'd participated in a number of sports throughout the school year, and the school's student council president two years running. Her parents had been on top of the world as they'd watched her give her Valedictory address at her Commencement ceremony, and hadn't minded at all that she'd started University that fall without declaring a major. *So much promise,* everyone had said. *Such an incredible future she had before her.*

Emily wondered idly what those same people would say if they could see her now, a forty-three-year -old, unmarried college drop-out standing in the kitchen of her parents' house, getting ready to stuff a turkey. Not exactly a representation of the promise they'd all seen in her. Not at all.

The thing of it was, Emily didn't mind one bit. She supposed even she would have been surprised to find that she actually enjoyed being up not long after dawn on a holiday weekend, enjoying the sleepy quiet of the house before the chaos of her family came crashing down the stairs to start their days. She sort of loved standing in her kitchen, getting ready to stuff a turkey. And she definitely adored the chaos of her family. In fact, the truth was, looking back on everything, if it had been up to her, Emily wouldn't have had it any other way.

The silence upstairs was broken by the light click of a door opening, followed by the sound of Trick's footsteps coming down the stairs. Seconds later, he was at her feet, saying hello, and after a quick lap at his water bowl, he padded over to the front door, tail wagging in anticipation. That meant that Samantha was up, at least. Her guess confirmed a few minutes later, when Emily heard Sam's footfalls on the stairs, and the subsequent greeting she was receiving from an excited, bouncing Trick.

Moments later, Sam strolled into the kitchen, pulling on her jacket and yanking the fridge door open to peer inside. Not seeing what she was looking for, she closed the door again and straightened up, watching her sister work.

"Morning, Em," she said, selecting instead an apple from a basket on the counter to take with her while she took the dog for a walk.

"Good morning, Samie," Emily responded, smiling at her. "Did you sleep okay?"

"Like a baby," Sam replied. She glanced back at the doorway as they heard Sarah making her way down the hall to the stairs. "Listen, Em, I was sorta wondering..." Knowing what was coming, Emily casually cut her off before she could finish her question.

"Of course Sarah can come with us today," she shrugged nonchalantly. "Wouldn't be right without her there, too, would it?" Sam grinned gratefully at her and grabbed her from behind, hugging her tightly.

"Thanks so much, Em," she enthused. "It'll be so great, but I wanted to make sure it was okay with you and Jules, too!" Emily returned her sister's smile.

"It's more than okay, kiddo," she replied. "It's pretty much perfect."

Sarah entered the kitchen then, and sauntered over to give Emily a hug and a sleepy smile before helping herself to an apple, as well. Emily smiled again as the girls grabbed Trick's leash and headed out the front door. Jules would be up soon, too, and between the two of them, all of the prep work for dinner would be done in time for them to still have a few solid hours for pumpkin shopping before they had to be back at the house to start cooking dinner. Emily glanced out of the window over the kitchen sink. The sun was up and seemingly hadn't burned off all of its summer heat quite yet. From the looks of things, it was going to be a very nice day.

*   *   *

Samantha and Trick led Sarah down to the bike path that ran along the bank of the river. It was one of Trick's favourite places to walk, as it was Sam's, and she was eager to show its quiet beauty to Sarah. Sam was sure that Sarah had her own favourite quiet spots when she was growing up, and Sam had been no different. They were just harder to find when you lived in the city. Despite the increasing warmth of the day, the area was deserted this early, and the two women walked hand in hand in near silence for awhile, while Trick ran on ahead, sniffing at everything and turning to check on the girls if they started to lag behind. Sam reveled in the peaceful serenity of the moment, and squeezed Sarah's hand contentedly. Sarah sighed happily.

"It feels more like it's spring than fall today, that's for sure," she observed dreamily. Sam nodded.

"Except for the leaves...they are falling instead of opening." Sam looked at the colours around her, noticing that there weren't as many left on the trees after all of the wind and rain from the night before. "Jules says that Dad used to tell us that, when the last leaf fell from the trees, that meant that summer had gone to sleep until next year, and that winter was officially here. We used to spend hours down here some years, counting the leaves that were left, so that we'd be ready when winter came." She glanced over at Sarah, who was smiling back at her, listening. Sam grinned at her before continuing.

"The Collins Family," she shook her head, "we have a bunch of crazy little traditions. The one today is the biggest, really...or, part of the biggest, anyway. It's something we've always done, and it's important that we keep doing it, I think.

See, we all go together to this pumpkin farm, and we each pick out a pumpkin to carve up for Halloween. Then, on the actual day, before the sun goes down, we get together and carve our pumpkins. It's pretty fun, and...it's been known to get a little competitive, from time to time." Sam blushed sheepishly for a moment, then continued.

"We each carve our own, and put candles in them, and then as the sun sets, we take two of them to the cemetery, one each for Mom and Dad, see?" She glanced again at Sarah, who nodded. "We take them and we talk to them...just kinda...catch them up on our year, you know? And then we leave them there, the pumpkins, with the candles in them, to keep away any evil spirits that might try to disturb their rest." Sam blushed again. "It sounds dumb, but that's what Jack-o'-Lanterns were for, originally, you know. Back in olden times...or, something like that..." Sam trailed off and looked at the ground as they walked.

"What about the third one?" Sarah asked curiously. Sam looked over at her from the corner of her eye.

"What?"

"The third pumpkin," Sarah explained. "You said you each carve one, but only two go to watch over your parents. There are three of you, so what happens to the third one?"

"Ah," Sam smiled. "We take turns, each year. The third pumpkin stays at the house. We light it up at night, with a candle, and put it in the window for them. It's to let them know that we're thinking of them, that we love them, and to help light their way home." Sam shrugged self-consciously. "This year it's my turn to carve that one. And," she said, stopping to look Sarah in the eye, "maybe it can be your turn, too, if you'll come?"

Tears welled up in Sarah's eyes. Sam looked like she was holding her breath, as though afraid of what her answer would be. Sarah had never seen her look quite so vulnerable before, and it made her heart ache. She leaned forward and kissed Samantha deeply.

"Of course I will come," she whispered, "It would be my sincere honour." Unable to speak, Sam simply hugged her tightly, and the two remained like that, locked in a warm embrace, for a few moments longer.

They parted as Trick trotted back to see what was taking them so long. The women laughed and scratched his ears, Sam promising that he could go on ahead; that they were right behind him.

"Let's head home, boy," she said. "We've got some pumpkins to pick out!"

~7~

Julie gazed idly out the window, barely registering the fall scenery flying past her as the car headed to the pumpkin farm. She was exhausted, having barely slept at all the night before, so Emily was driving, while Sam, Sarah and Trick reclined together in the back. The farm was maybe only about a half hour's drive outside of the city, but already it seemed like a whole other world. Paved parking lots and concrete buildings had been replaced by trees and fields, dotted here and there with farm houses and barns. Unbroken by high-rises and condo buildings, the blue sky now seemed enormous in comparison, with white fluffy clouds billowing by, intermittently interrupting the bright sunshine of late morning. It was a gorgeous October day.

Julie began reflecting again on the events of the night before. Something about it all was gnawing at her insides, but she couldn't quite put her finger on it. The look on Samantha's face just before she had bolted from the house had been sheer mortification mixed with dread, and ...something else. Julie struggled, but was unable to come up with a name to describe the range of emotions that has passed so rapidly across her sister's face. She wasn't even really sure as to what exactly had triggered Sam in the first place. What had Emily said? Something about Sam being a boy's name? Julie shook her head. That wasn't quite right, no. It had been something about their parents wanting a boy...

Julie frowned. That didn't make any sense. Sam knew that she was loved, by both of the parents, and by her older sisters, as well. There was no reason for her to ever entertain the idea that she hadn't been wanted and loved for exactly who she was. She'd grown up hearing and even participating in such jokes from time to time, because she'd known, as they all did, that the very idea was ludicrous. And yet, for some reason, it had set her off and running, anyway. Just like she had run the first time;

the night their parents died.

Julie remembered that night like it was yesterday. She could still feel the panic rise in her throat as she and Sam had rounded the corner onto their street, and had seen the flashing lights of the police car, along with half the neighbourhood, right outside their house. At first she'd thought there was a fire...she'd dropped everything and ran, fearing for Emily because they'd left her alone to handle the trick-or-treaters all by herself while she and Sam had gone on a hunt for their own sugary loot. She'd slowed when she realized that it was just the one car, and that no fire trucks or alarms seemed to be part of the picture.

She'd seen the look on Emily's face, however, and an icy understanding had come over her almost instantly. Their parents were gone.

Julie had gradually become dimly aware that Samantha was terrified. Too young to understand what was going on, she'd been standing off to one side, watching everyone with those wide troubled blue eyes she had, and twisting her sleeve cuff nervously, seemingly afraid to intrude, and yet looking so very tiny and alone at that moment. Julie had gone to her, gathered her small, shivering body up in her arms, and delivered the terrible news to her as gently but as honestly as she could.

Sam had gone into a sort of shock...she had stared at Julie, and then Emily, and had not made a sound. Huge crocodile tears slid silently down her cheeks while her sisters continued speaking with the police, but she hadn't said a single word. She just kept twisting her sleeve, as though trying to process everything as best she could on her own, without having to bother anyone for help.

Then, seemingly out of nowhere, she'd made a small, choking sound in the back of her throat. Julie had looked at her, and had seen that same look on her face as the one she'd had last night...a mix of mortification, dread and something Julie still wasn't sure about. Sam's face had flushed red, eyes filled with tears, and she'd been gone, her little legs carrying her out of of the house and into the night before any of the rest of them could react.

A shocked moment passed, and then Emily and Julie had been on their feet, springing after her as quickly as they could. The girls had been frantic, screaming Sam's name into the dark, unsure as to the direction she had taken. Em had suddenly grown calm, and turned to Julie, saying that she was going to go look for Sam, but that Julie should stay at the house in case she came back. Julie was beside herself with worry, but did as she was told. She busied herself with mundane tasks, keeping one eye on the clock. The female police officer, Pam, had stayed with her, helping in any way she could. The two had put tea on, as to Julie it seemed like it would be the only way to take the sudden chill out of her soul. The young male officer...Brian something? Ryan? - had accompanied Emily on her hunt for Sam, though Julie had always suspected that he'd mostly just followed her and kept an eye on things, rather than actually being allowed to go *with* her. Emily had been on a mission that night and, instinctively, everyone had known to just keep their distance and let her do what she'd needed to do.

They seemed to have been gone forever, but Julie knew from checking the clock every twenty seconds or so, that it had really only been just under half an hour before she heard their footsteps on the porch, and she had rushed to let them in.

Emily was carrying Samantha in her arms, almost cradling her like a baby. The girl had nearly fallen asleep, her tear-stained face a blotchy red, both from crying and from the chill in the air that evening. And she was sucking her thumb.

Without a word, Emily had carried Sam all the way upstairs, and put her to bed, before rejoining the others downstairs. Neither she nor Sam ever spoke about what had happened, or where she'd found Sam that night. It became almost like it had never happened.

Almost.

Later that night, after the police and the neighbours had all left, and after the older girls had also gone to bed, Julie had awoken to find Sam snuggled in bed next to her, still sucking her thumb, and curled up in the tiniest ball possible. Julie had dropped an arm over her, tucked the comforter in around the both of them, and went back to sleep. For weeks after the funeral, it was the same routine: Sam would go to bed, and Julie would wake up to find her sleeping next to her hours later. Sam never spoke of it, and Julie had just let her be. One morning, after Julie had slept soundly through the night, she awoke to find herself alone in bed, and had checked to discover that Sam had slept through in her own bed once again, and that was the end of it. She'd often wake Julie if she had a nightmare, for she'd had many, but she'd always, since then, spent the night in her own bed. Whatever she'd needed from Julie those first nights, she'd needed no longer.

Julie smiled ruefully. Her baby sister had always seemed so much littler than she and Emily were. *And now I'm the short one*, she thought, rolling her eyes. *Nice.* Julie glanced in the side mirror, catching a glimpse of the girls in the back seat, which returned her to the journey at hand. She hoped no one had noticed her mind wandering, but then, she supposed, no one would really bother. This was the time of year when all of their minds often drifted to other things. All the same, however, Julie didn't want to miss anything by living too much in the past, so she turned her attention to the present conversation going on around her.

Sam had started teasing Sarah about her small town life, asking very pointed questions every time she spotted a cow or a corn field. Julie wished she felt better so that she could join in, but she was so tired, and she could still feel the pain deep down inside her, waiting on the periphery of her senses, no doubt intending to pounce again at any time. She was finding it difficult to focus on anything. She could see Em occasionally glancing over at her curiously, as she drove, but thankfully she opted not to ask any questions right then. Julie instead retreated inside her mind, turning her thoughts toward how and when she was ever going to tell her sisters about her disease. *My disease*, she thought, screwing up her face. *Like I have ownership of it, or something.*

She did not want to tell them this weekend, she knew. Nor did she want to ruin their Halloween tradition with such bad news, either. There was a very good chance that she wouldn't make it to next year, and it was important that this year go smoothly, in case it really was their last one all together like this. She did, however, want to tell them both in person, not while Sam was away at school. And it had to be soon. Emily already suspected that something was going on, and even Sarah had noticed that there was something different about her, and they had only just met. Christmas would be too far away, as things were declining rapidly now, and they would have already long since guessed that something was wrong, putting two and two together on their own. Julie sighed, turning the issue over in her mind. It would have to be Halloween, she decided. But not until after they had done what they needed to do. Halloween was on a Saturday this year, so Sam wouldn't be leaving again until at least the Sunday, if not an extra day later.

Julie smiled as the car erupted in laughter at something Sarah had said, retorting to another of Samantha's jokes, then returned to watching, unseeing, as the scenery flew by outside. Everything was moving so quickly, it seemed to her now. Julie sighed again, her mind made up. She would tell them then. On the Sunday. For better or for worse.

*   *   *

Emily wandered amid the many pumpkins for sale, eyeing the various shapes and sizes, and keeping watch for the one she would choose to carve into her masterpiece this year. The others were on similar hunts nearby, each woman bending to inspect her options closely before deciding whether to move on. She could hear Samantha explaining the secrets to choosing the perfect specimen to Sarah, who stood listening and nodding, a twinkle in her eye. Emily could tell that Sarah was thrilled to have been asked along, and Emily was just as thrilled to have her there. Something about it all just seemed right.

She stood still, an unseasonably warm sun beating down on her, surveying the variety of pumpkins in her immediate vicinity, keeping a mental checklist of possibilities going as she did so. She had narrowed it down to a shortlist of about five or six various opportunities, but she needed to be sure. She wanted this one to be perfect.

Emily glanced over to where Julie was standing, off to one side, quietly working her way down one side of the enclosure, and occasionally taking a step or two toward the centre, having a closer look at a pumpkin or two, then gingerly stepping back to the fringes. Emily frowned, watching her sister. Something definitely wasn't right. Normally, Julie would be practically dancing through the middle of the pumpkin patch, wanting to be sure she didn't miss a thing. Choosing her pumpkin each year was one of her favourite things, from the time they had been children, and it still continued to be to this day. Yet today, Julie was picking through the patch cautiously, as though afraid she would break something. It was very unlike her.

Emily stood still, watching Jules, frowning again as she did so. She hadn't seemed to be herself in the car on the way over, either. She'd appeared to be withdrawn; reserved. Emily had quietly asked if she was okay, and Jules had simply brushed her concern away, saying that she was just tired; that everything was fine. Thinking back, Emily realized that Julie had been tired a lot lately, and looking at her now, in the sunlight and bright colours of the pumpkin farm in fall, she appeared paler and perhaps even thinner than she'd been even just a few weeks ago. Julie definitely looked to be tired, but she seemed to be a lot more than that, as well. She looked entirely worn out. Emily had the sudden feeling that, given half a chance, Julie would have happily curled up on the bare ground and fallen asleep right then and there.

She's not okay, Emily thought, feeling panic rise in her chest. *Something's wrong. Could it be...? Please, God, no...not that...*

Fighting the urge to confront Julie right away, Emily reasoned that she could always get her alone later on, and quietly get to the bottom of whatever it was. She was probably just coming down with the flu, or something, but Emily figured a trip to the doctor couldn't hurt. And since it was the holiday weekend, it could wait until next week, at least. She took a deep breath, releasing it slowly.

Relax, she told herself, attempting to quell the nagging feeling that she needed to do something right away. *One thing at a time.*

Julie looked up and caught her staring in her direction, so Emily smiled faintly, lifting one hand in a casual wave. Jules returned the wave, grinning, and in that moment, Emily saw her sister back to her usual self, inwardly breathing a silent sigh of relief. She had no sooner turned back to the very serious task of choosing her perfect pumpkin for carving when, suddenly, she heard her name being called. Turning in the direction it was coming from, Emily took a moment to recognize the man slowly but enthusiastically making his way in her direction. Dressed in faded jeans and a tight black t-shirt, a ball cap pulled slightly askew atop his head, he couldn't have looked less like himself if he'd tried. The only thing giving him away was his seemingly standard issue sunglasses.

"Officer M...Ryan," Emily stammered, suddenly feeling self-conscious and nervous. "What are you doing here?"

Flashing her his trademark crooked grin, Ryan stumbled once, recovered, and landed not quite gracefully in front of her; one hand on his hip, the other nonchalantly picking at his fingernails with his thumb.

"Oh, you know, I was just in the neighbourhood..." he yawned, feigning boredom, then grinned again. "Just kidding. Stake-out. Very top secret. Very hush-hush cop-like stuff," he whispered in mock seriousness. Emily, wide-eyed, matched his cloak-and-dagger tone, and leaned in close, also lowering her voice to a whisper.

"I think one of the gang of pumpkins over to the left may be suspicious. I heard them earlier saying that they could smell a cop from a mile away, so you should be careful." She caught a hint of his aftershave on the breeze, and was momentarily distracted. "I mean we...um...we wouldn't want a stampede, or anything, correct?" Ryan smiled at her again, and she groaned inwardly.

Note to Self, she thought ruefully. *Stop talking - right now. Good grief.*

Thankfully, Emily had already completely forgotten what she was saying. Ryan had removed his glasses; his brown eyes now squinting at her thoughtfully. An awkward moment passed between them, but was broken when he spoke again.

"Actually, I'm here with my sister and her kids," he confessed. "I was told my presence had been requested by the young ones, but apparently they were more interested in whether or not I would let them 'play the siren' than they were in seeing me! Their enthusiasm for seeing me dropped dramatically when I showed up with my own car." He grimaced and rolled his eyes. "Some people's kids..." he sighed, shaking his head, as Emily laughed. He peered at her again. "How about you?" he asked. "What brings you all the way out here?"

Emily glanced around her, feeling momentarily stunned. In her unexpected pleasure at running into Ryan, she had sort of forgotten for a moment where she was, why she was there...and who she was with. Too late, she realized that Julie, Sam and Sarah had all noticed her chatting with Ryan, and were obviously, but unobtrusively, all trying to sidle even closer to no doubt investigate the mysterious man talking to their sister. She might be able to divert Sam and Sarah's attention, Emily knew, but Julie would be impossible. She would recognize him right away, and would very likely be suspicious. Emily wasn't sure what to do, but there was no sense in worrying about something she couldn't control. She would just have to play it by ear. She met Ryan's eyes and gave him her best and biggest smile.

"I'm here with my sisters," she grinned, jerking her thumb casually over her shoulder to indicate that they were right nearby. As, she knew, they would be by now. "We have a sort of tradition, for this time of year." Ryan's smile faltered slightly, and Emily thought she saw him suddenly flush pink a little bit, though it was difficult to tell for sure in the sunshine. He looked at her, then, genuine concern evident in his brown eyes.

"Oh," he said, lowering his voice somewhat. "I'm sorry, I didn't mean to interrupt ..." his voice trailed off, and his eyes darted off to one side, behind her. Without turning around, she felt Julie at her elbow, a mere second before she saw her hand extend in Ryan's direction.

"Hi there," she cut in smoothly. "I'm Julie, Emily's sist- ... do I know you?"

Here we go, then, Emily thought to herself with a sigh.

"Jules, this is Ryan Mullen," she explained. "*Officer* Ryan Mullen, you remember?" At Julie's slow nod of recognition, she continued. "Ryan, this is my sister, Julie."

The pair shook hands, and Ryan grinned briefly at Emily once again before turning his attention just off to her right. Emily stifled a chuckle and looked at the ground. Ryan leaned forward, hand extended in greeting.

"And you must be Samantha," he said easily. "You're a lot bigger than I remember," he grinned, reaching to pet Trick as he sniffed around Ryan's shoe. "I'm Ryan. Your sister has told me a lot about you. Good to see you again!"

"Thanks...I think?" Sam laughed. She looked from Ryan to Emily and back again, her brow wrinkling slightly in confusion. "I'm sorry, I don't think I remember..."

"You were still pretty young the last time I saw you," Ryan said effortlessly. "I wouldn't expect you to remember me, but I remember you...with added help from Emily here, of course. She keeps me updated on the lot of you."

"Does she?" Julie muttered thoughtfully, gazing intently at her older sister. Emily swallowed, gluing her smile back in place.

"Samie, Officer Mullen...Ryan...was one of the police officers who came to help us the night of Mom and Dad's accident," she explained, trying to alter the course of the conversation a little. "He came with us to court all those times, during the trial, remember?" Nervously aware that she sounded as though she was speaking to a child, Emily nevertheless watched Samantha, waiting as she processed this particular piece of information. Sam was staring at Ryan, and Emily could practically see the variety of emotions flitting across the girl's face. She wondered how much Sam even really remembered about that night and the following months, and was mildly worried about how seeing Ryan now might effect her, particularly after the episode she'd gone through the night before. Realizing that she was holding her breath, Emily let it out slowly, watching.

"Su-ure," Samantha responded slowly. "I remember you." She continued staring at him another moment, then blinked, and self-consciously shook her head. "I'm sorry, Officer," she said, reaching back to grab Sarah's hand and pulling her forward to stand next to her. "I'm being rude...this is my girlfriend, Sarah."

Emily thought she noticed the slightest trace of hesitation in the introduction, but she was proud of Sam for taking such a huge step after having only just openly spoken about her feelings for Sarah with both of her sisters the night before. And if the way she beamed at Sam before reaching to shake Ryan's hand was any indication, it looked to Emily as though Sarah felt exactly the same way.

"It's nice to meet you, Officer Mullen," Sarah said, smiling. Ryan grinned back at her.

"It's lovely to meet you, as well, Sarah," he said, winking at Emily from the corner of his eye. "But please, just call me Ryan." Sarah accepted the request with a gracious nod, then stepped back, and took Sam's hand, pulling her back the way they had come. Trick followed along close behind, tail wagging furiously, careful not to let either of his girls out of his sight.

"Come honey," Sarah said with a chuckle, "let us return to the pumpkin patch from whence we came!" Sam seemed about to object, but Sarah gave her a look that convinced her to go along, regardless.

"It was nice to see you...Ryan," Sam yelled back over her shoulder as Sarah dragged her back to their search. Ryan waved good-naturedly and turned to Emily and Julie.

"And so," he said to the two women, turning more serious, "how are you holding up? I imagine that this must be a difficult time of year for you all." He shook his head, smiling almost as if to himself. "Honestly, your resilience and strength, from the time I met you through to right now, has never ceased to amaze and impress me," he said sincerely.

"Thank you, Ryan," Emily began, but Julie suddenly cut her off.

"Yes, thank you, Ryan," she said. "That's a very kind thing to say." Julie hesitated for a moment, looking from one to the other of them, a strange, unreadable expression on her face. "I have to go," she said abruptly. "It was good to see you, again, Ryan. And Em, I'll catch up with you in a few minutes. Don't wander off!" And with that, she, too, was gone, stepping gingerly over and around pumpkins as though she were in the midst of some strange, themed obstacle course.

Emily glanced back at Ryan, noticed that he was looking at her again, a twinkle of bemusement in his brown eyes, and ducked her head shyly for a moment, unsure of what to say. Ryan broke the awkward silence for her.

"So," he began. "I...um...so, I know that this might seem a little..." He shook his head, took a deep breath, looked away, and started again. "I was wondering if you'd maybe go out with me sometime," he blurted, turning a definite crimson under the bright sun. "For...dinner?" Ryan glanced back at her, no doubt trying to gauge her reaction. Pause. "Maybe?"

Emily stared at him, blinked twice, and then looked away. She was not at all used to this. She'd dated before, of course, but this was someone...this was a man who, in at least one way, knew her better than anyone. She found herself at once elated, excited, terrified and incredibly nervous all at once. It was like being asked to the school prom, only with adults playing the roles of awkward teenagers. She thought it was ridiculous, but at the same time, was completely unable to settle the butterflies that had suddenly appeared to have taken over her stomach. She shook her head, trying to get her bearings. What was that line people always used in the movies, to carry them through moments like this? Emily's mind fumbled about for an answer, and just when she'd about given up hope of ever being able to carry on a normal conversation with anyone again, let alone with this particular man, she found and seized upon the words she'd been looking for.

"I'd love to," Emily replied with a polite smile. She exhaled slowly...she'd been holding her breath again. Ryan grinned suddenly, lighting up like a child on Christmas morning.

"Great," he said, his attempt at seeming casual completely undermined by his obvious relief and excitement regarding her answer. "I'll give you a call...Friday, maybe?" He turned at the sound of his name being called, and the sight of two younger children making their way through the holiday weekend crowd prompted him to check his watch.

"Oh gosh," he said with a start. "It's later than I thought. Time flies," he grinned with a wink, making it Emily's turn to blush. "I have to go," he said. "But I will call you. Friday, okay?" He hugged her awkwardly, and started to walk toward the children, watching her over his shoulder." Emily found herself sort of saddened by the idea of his departure so soon.

"Friday it is," she agreed. "Wait," she called suddenly, waiting until he turned back before continuing. "Do you even have my number?" Ryan laughed, then spread his hands out in a self-satisfied gesture.

"Of course," he chuckled. "Have I ever mentioned that I'm a cop?" He grinned, winked yet again, and turned to lavish attention on the two children who'd finally made their way over to him. He picked one up and ruffled the other's hair, picking his way over to where their mother, his sister, stood watching. She glanced at Emily, then said something to Ryan before turning to head back in the opposite direction from where Emily stood.

Ryan raised his hand in a farewell salute, but Emily didn't see it.

She was too busy smiling giddily at the bright orange pumpkins scattered across the ground before her, trying to remember where she was and what she'd been doing before he'd called out to her. Emily smiled again, no longer able to focus on the task at hand. She chuckled again, quietly.

"Friday it is," she muttered happily.

~8~

Sarah watched Sam as she laid out three possible pumpkin choices, and carefully inspected each one, explaining to Sarah each step of the thought process involved in choosing the perfect pumpkin as she went along, almost as though Sarah had never carved a Jack-o'-Lantern before. Sarah smiled patiently as she watched Samantha work, while Trick pawed briefly at a stick he found in the dirt nearby. She supposed, in some respects, this would be like learning to carve one all over again, as this was the first time it would really matter. This was the first time she would ever carve it with a meaning; a purpose. And in that, Samantha had most of her lifetime's worth of experience, wherein Sarah had exactly none. Though she was fairly certain she could handle the pressure of this being her 'first time', she nevertheless watched and listened closely to Sam's instructions. She loved how passionate Samantha could get about things that really meant something to her. It was part of her charm.

And really, Sarah thought, grinning fondly down at her girlfriend, *it is pretty damn adorable.*

"You have to check the weight of it," Sam was explaining, "and test the angle, you know?" She looked up at Sarah to make sure she was still paying attention. "You definitely don't want it to roll over, or something, once it's all carved and lit up, see?" Sam nudged one of her already-discarded pumpkins and it easily rolled over onto its side, bobbing gently in the dirt before stopping, its top stem now seeming all askew.

"And you want it to be thick, but not *too* thick, 'cause that makes it harder to carve really detailed stuff sometimes." Sam glanced up at Sarah again. "And, if you already know what you want to carve, it's best, because then you can pick out the best canvas on which to display your

88

work, so to speak. It's...like...art...why are you smiling like that? Do I amuse you?" She asked, her huge blue eyes dancing. Sarah laughed.

"No, baby," she giggled lightly. "Or...well, yes, but not in the way you think!" she added quickly, reacting to the expression of mock indignation that crossed Sam's face. "I just think you're cute, is all," she winked. "Tell me more. Please."

Sarah listened as Sam explained about pumpkin defects and faults, and how they could be used in her favour, depending on what she wanted to carve. She could tell that Samantha was fishing, trying desperately to find out if Sarah knew what she would be carving, or not. Sarah knew exactly what she was going to do, of course. But she had no intention of spoiling the surprise for Sam, so she maintained her tight-lipped policy to the letter, smiling with a gleam in her eye the entire time.

Once Sam had given her all of the advice she could think of, and had begun the process of narrowing down her short-list to just one sole pumpkin-y winner, Sarah gazed around those remaining in the pumpkin area, looking for Emily and Julie. She spotted Emily first, crouching down and closely inspecting a more oblong-shaped pumpkin, seemingly no longer aware of the world around her. The police officer, Ryan, had left after a brief, but rather interesting-looking, conversation with Emily, and now she was alone again, completely focused on choosing her perfect pumpkin. Sarah nearly laughed out loud when she saw Emily give the oblong pumpkin a nudge, then nodding in satisfaction as it managed to remain upright. She doubted if either of them really knew it, but Samantha and Emily were near carbon-copies of one another, with the difference in their ages being the only real distance between them. It was so obvious to her, watching them, and she fervently hoped, for their sakes, that they would someday be able to see it, as well.

Sarah watched as Emily scooped up her chosen pumpkin, and turned to survey the area, no doubt looking to check on her sisters' progress in the hunt. With the sun in her eyes, it was difficult to see Sarah and Sam, though they were not too far off from where she was standing. Despite the bright sun, however, she managed to spot them first, and lifted her free hand in a brief wave when she noticed Sarah watching her. Sarah waved back, then pointed at Sam and gave a brief thumbs-up, to signal that they were nearly ready, as well. Both women then turned away to search for Julie.

Sarah saw her first, standing in the shade at the far end of the pumpkin enclosure, leaning awkwardly against a tree. A rather lopsided pumpkin lay at an angle at her feet, and she was staring, unseeing, toward the ground in front of her. She looked to be sweating, despite the chill of the mid-October air, and seemed to be having difficulty breathing. Alarmed, Sarah looked to Emily, intending to alert her to Julie's location, but realized immediately that Emily had already spotted her sister. And from the way she stood frozen in place, staring over at Julie, Emily did not like what she saw. A moment later, she was on the move, crossing the pumpkin area quickly with her long, determined strides. Sarah picked up the round pumpkin she'd had her eye on from the beginning and turned to Sam, who had finally chosen her own carving canvas.

"Sam," Sarah said, trying to keep the alarm out of her voice. "Come on, sweetie. We have to go." Sam looked up at her then, seeing the expression of concern on her face, stood quickly and looked around, her wide eyes searching the area as quickly as she could.

"What happened?" she asked, instantly worried. "What's wrong?" Sarah took her hand and pointed across the pumpkin area, to where Emily had already reached Julie and had an arm around her sister, talking quietly to her as she tried to determine what was wrong. Sam's eyes got wider still as she spotted them, and she immediately took off, running toward the tree where they stood as quickly as she could without falling over anyone along the way. Trick bounded along behind her, enjoying the sudden freedom he had to run. Sarah scooped up the chosen pumpkin that Sam had left behind and, carrying both, hurried after them.

"I'm fine," she heard Julie say as she approached. "Honest. I likely just ate something that didn't agree with me, or something. Seriously, I'll be fine." She smiled ruefully. "Don't worry."

Emily and Samantha didn't appear to be convinced but, at Julie's insistence, they agreed to let it drop for the time being, on the condition that they pay for the pumpkins and head home immediately so that Julie could get some rest. She definitely looked to Sarah like she needed it. Her face was pale; her blue eyes dulled from the pain she was experiencing. It seemed as though she could barely stand on her own and, as Sam stooped to retrieve Julie's pumpkin from the ground, Emily gently took her arm and started to lead her toward the checkout area. They hadn't gotten far before Julie stopped them. She looked around nervously, licking her lips.

"Listen, would it be okay if you guys get this one, and I just wait in the car? I think I need to sit down..."

"Of course," Emily agreed immediately, digging her keys out from her purse. Julie, one hand pressed to her abdomen, reached her other hand out to accept the keys from Emily, but Emily held them out to Sarah, instead.

"Give those to Sam and I," she said, gesturing to the pumpkins in Sarah's arms, "and take her to the car, please?" Julie seemed about to object but, after a quick look at the serious expressions on her sisters' faces, thought the better of it, and remained silent. Sarah nodded, handed her pumpkin charges over in exchange for the car keys, and took a gentle but firm hold of Julie's arm. She looked down at Trick, who was standing in the middle of them all, looking mildly confused and concerned that they seemed to be splitting up, thereby making his job that much more difficult.

"You comin' or stayin'?" she asked him. Trick, tail still wagging, looked back and forth between the women, panting in dog-like contemplation. Sarah bent over and gave him a brief scratch behind the ears, then straightened, smiling. "Stay with Sam," she said. "We'll meet you at the car." At the mention of the word, 'car', Trick's ears perked up even more, but he held his ground, waiting to see which direction Samantha would head in before he made a move.

"See you in a few minutes," Sarah called over her shoulder to Emily and Sam as she turned and began steering Julie back toward the distant parking lot.

Sarah didn't waste any time locating the car once they'd reached the parking lot. She could feel Julie's shaking steps and wanted to get her to a spot where she could sit down comfortably and rest as quickly as possible. They arrived at the car and Sarah unlocked the passenger side door, bending in to recline the seat slightly, then stepped aside to let Julie climb inside.

Julie leaned back against the seat, and closed her eyes.

"Thanks, Sarah," she said quietly. "Hey, leave the door open a minute, would you? The breeze feels good..."

Sarah obliged, looking from Julie, reclining with her eyes still closed, back to the direction they'd just come from, watching for the girls' return. Julie seemed to be more comfortable, and her breathing evened out, becoming less labored. She looked exhausted; worn out. Sarah checked again for the girls and, not seeing them, took a deep breath herself, and let it out slowly.

"You're not really okay, are you," she said quietly. It was not a question. Julie didn't respond, just continued to sit with her eyes closed, breathing slowly. Sarah thought she may have fallen asleep, but then her lips moved, her voice little more than a whisper in the breeze.

"No."

Momentarily stunned, Sarah exhaled, unsure what to say next. She'd known the answer, but hadn't thought that Jules would admit to it at all, let alone to her. Let alone with such simple candor. Sarah bit her lip anxiously, and responded in the only way she could think to.

"I'm sorry," she whispered. Julie opened her eyes, looked directly at Sarah, and then over her shoulder. Sarah didn't even have time to turn around.

"Sorry for what?" Sam asked, reaching to retrieve the keys and tossing them to Emily. She looked at Julie briefly, then met Sarah's eyes with a questioning look and lowered her voice. "How's she doing?"

"She's right here," Julie groaned, sitting up in her seat with a grimace. "And she can speak for herself, thanks." Sam looked at her.

"Okay, sorry," she apologized. "You seemed kinda out of it, and I didn't want to bother you." Samantha shrugged, turning her attention back to Sarah, her concern evident on her face. "Sorry for what?"

Sarah paused, glancing at Julie. The woman was gazing steadily back at her, her eyes silently pleading with Sarah not to reveal anything about what had been said. Sarah felt guilty keeping anything from Sam, but this, she felt, was not her secret to tell. Julie would talk to her sisters when she was ready, and Sarah knew better than to try and push that agenda, particularly when she really had no idea of the details involved. Sarah looked her girlfriend in the eye and answered truthfully, at least, for the most part.

"I'm sorry that she's feeling so ill on such a gorgeous day," she said simply. "And even though you seem to be feeling a bit *better*," she said, giving Julie a pointed look, "I think maybe we should get you home now." She turned back to Sam. "Don't you?" Sarah couldn't tell if Sam just didn't believe her, or if she was really more concerned about her sister than she was letting on, but her lips pressed together in thought for a moment, considering. Then she glanced briefly to Emily, before nodding once and turning to open the back door, while Emily popped the trunk so they could pack the pumpkins and be on their way.

Sarah met Julie's eye once more before climbing into the back seat behind her, and saw the thinly veiled gratitude hidden there. She smiled tightly, touched her shoulder lightly, and got into the car. Trick leapt in right behind her, happily reclaiming his spot in the middle of it all, followed by Sam, after pausing to push Julie's door shut for her. As Emily got in, checked to make sure everyone was buckled in, and started the car, Sarah reached over to take Sam's hand and give her a reassuring squeeze. She exhaled gratefully at the return squeeze, and smiled over at her girlfriend...just in time to receive Trick's tongue right in the nose as he gave her face an excited lick of greeting. Sam chuckled quietly, but no one spoke as the car pulled out of the parking area and headed toward the highway. By the time they got there, Julie had already fallen asleep, and Sarah stared quietly out of the window, deeply troubled by all that she had learned.

*   *   *

Samantha finished setting everyone's place at the table, and paused to survey her handiwork. She had a brief fleeting memory of her mother teaching her about where everything went, and smiled to herself. She'd been barely tall enough to see over the tabletop, but she'd been so eager to learn. Her sisters were always helping their mother in the kitchen, and Sam had wanted desperately to do her part; to share in the time they were all spending together. In tears, she'd begged her mother to let her help one evening as they were preparing dinner. Her mother had smiled, kissed the top of her head, and taken her aside, to a corner of the kitchen. It was there, on a rickety TV tray table, that Samantha had first learned the basic rules of table setting. Her mother had helped her set up one place on the small table, and then had sent her on a quest to set the big table in the dining room where they would all be eating together a short time later. Sam had diligently memorized the place setting, making it a picture in her mind. She had then, carefully and on tiptoes, recreated the picture on the big table, one at a time, until she'd had five places set. Her mother had inspected each one closely while Sam stood nearby, nervously awaiting her verdict. Sam had held her breath as her mother had turned to look at her, and released it only when her mother's familiar smile had lit up her face once more. She'd scooped Sam up in a hug, and showed her how the table looked from an angle someone taller could see it from. All of the place settings had been off to one side of where they were supposed to be (in her determination to get it right. Sam hadn't thought to move the chairs out of her way first), but they were all correct, exactly how her mother had shown her. From that night on, and for several years at least, setting the table had become Samantha's job, a role she'd never really grown tired of, even after she'd grown up and moved out of the house. It had been her rite of passage. She'd found her place among the women of her family at last.

Now, being that she was a guest, everyone had staunchly refused all of Sarah's offers to help, insisting instead that she take up a spot in the kitchen that would allow her to remain a part of the conversation, but that would still keep her out of the way while the sisters prepared their Thanksgiving feast. Sam had even graciously promised to let Sarah clean up after them all, to which she'd received quick glare accompanied by a dish towel snap from Emily. Returning to the kitchen after having set the table, however, Sam paused in the doorway, smirking at the sight of her girlfriend hard at work creating a mixed green salad. She rolled her eyes at her sisters, identical expressions of innocence plastered all over their faces. She wished she was surprised.

"You're so weak," she sighed disappointedly, before crossing the room to kiss Sarah lightly on the cheek.

"Oh really?" Julie piped up, seeming to have a little more energy since taking a nap earlier in the day, after their return from the pumpkin farm. "Well, little sister, I'll have you know..." she paused as Sam looked at her expectantly, then sighed. "I got nothin'." She shook her head. "Em?"

"Shut the front door," Emily joked, using one of her favourite non-curse-word expressions. "And pass me the other oven mitt, would you, please?" Sam laughed, handed her sister the oven mitt she needed, and began carrying hot dishes of food out to the table. It was time to eat.

A short while later, all four women were seated around the table together. The chandelier had been dimmed, the candles had been lit, and everyone had a full glass of chardonnay in front of her. Emily raised her glass in a short toast.

"Happy Thanksgiving, everyone," she said, smiling as the sentiment was echoed by everyone in attendance, and clinking glasses were heard around the table. Trick was sprawled nearby, watching every movement as he conserved his energy for the moment the turkey was to be carved. Emily waited until everyone had tasted a sip of their wine before continuing. "Each year, before we begin our meal, we traditionally go around the table, and everyone lists at least one thing for which they are most thankful," she explained, more for Sarah's benefit than anything else. "That being said, because I am the eldest, I will start." Emily cleared her throat.

"I am thankful that we are all here, together; that my family is safe, all here under the same roof. All of us home, together, for this holiday. I am thankful for you, Jules, for teaching me about strength and courage, and for being my constant, my rock, and very best friend." Emily cleared her throat again.

"I am thankful for you, Samie, for showing me that being true to who you are is the only way to be truly happy in this world. I am so proud of you for having the courage to be yourself, and for finally finding a way to let people in enough to know you, and to love you for the kind, generous, and remarkably beautiful woman that you really are. *So* proud, baby sister," Emily breathed, shaking her head, as if to clear it.

"And I am thankful for you, Sarah, for being the kind of person who sees all of that and more in her. Thank you for being here, for sharing yourself with us, for taking care of our girl, and for making her so happy. You've found a rare person in our Samantha, and to me, that makes you a very rare person, as well. Welcome to our family." The women all raised their glasses again, and Sam quietly wiped a tear from her cheek. She no longer knew what she had expected from this weekend, but it certainly hadn't been *that*.

"My turn," Julie began in a quiet voice. She still seemed a little pale, even in the candlelight, Sam thought, but her eyes remained lively and alert, nonetheless. "Though that will be tough to top, so I won't even try - much." She smiled slightly, a gleam in her eye. "Sam, I, too, am so very proud of you, and I am unbelievably happy that you and Sarah have found one another. You look to me to be each other's match, and I couldn't have ever imagined a better partner for you, nor a better little sister, in you, for me. You know...when you aren't being a pest," she laughed.

"Emily, I don't think any of us will ever truly grasp the magnitude of what you gave up, and what you went through, to keep us all together. I look around this table, now, at the faces, at the food we've prepared, and at the home we've made, and I know that none of it would have been possible were it not for the unique and all-encompassing love that you have for us all. That you've always had. I know we are not the kind of family that anyone sets out to create, but we are all we have. And, honestly, Em...if they could see us now, I think Mom and Dad would be so very proud of you, as I am, and they would know without a doubt that they left us in very capable hands. You are more the sister, and all the parent, anyone could ever ask for. And don't let anyone, not even your own little inside voice, ever make you think any different. I love you, Em; I love you, Sam, and now I am growing to love you, too, Sarah. If I lived a thousand lifetimes, I don't think I could ever find anyone I would rather call sister, nor friend, than all of you. From the bottom of my heart, ladies, Happy Thanksgiving."

Samantha stared at her sisters, both of whom had now joined her and Sarah in wiping tears from their cheeks. While they had always, as Emily had explained, given short speeches of thanks prior to eating dinner each year, they hadn't usually been like *this*.

"Well," she said, having to clear her throat as well, now, "I guess

I'm thankful that Jules didn't *try* to top Em's speech!" Sam rolled her eyes as the others laughed lightly. "Truly, though, I do want to say..." Sam paused, her breath momentarily caught in her throat. "I - I want to say that I am thankful for everyone here at this table tonight. I am thankful to you, my sisters, because, while I don't have very many vivid memories left of Mom and Dad, I know that I wouldn't have any if you both hadn't worked so hard to keep them sort of alive for me. You never let me forget; not about them, and not about me. I grew up knowing them almost as though they'd been here the entire time and, more importantly, I grew up knowing I was loved, every moment of every day. Loved by them, and loved by you. Except maybe that time I drew on the walls in crayon, but regardless," Sam hesitated, chuckling, then turned to look at her sisters again. "Seriously, I am thankful to you for never letting me forget where I came from, or who I am. I am thankful for your love, and your support, and for everything you each gave up so that I could have a chance at something more. If it takes me the rest of my life, I swear to you that I will do right by the gift you have given me, and you'll know that it wasn't in vain; that it wasn't wasted."

Emily opened her mouth to speak, but Samantha cut her off.

"You are, both of you, the best parents I could have asked for, better sisters than I ever could have imagined, and two of the most amazing and beautiful women I will even have the honour of knowing. I am thankful to you both, just for keeping me." Sam choked back a sob, shook her head once, and took a deep, shaky breath.

"Sarah," she said quietly, "I am thankful for everything you are, for everything you have been, and for everything you will be. I am thankful for your smile, because it shows me that you are happy. I am thankful for your eyes when they look at me, because they show me that you see me for who I really am. I am thankful for your beautiful heart, because it is big enough, and generous enough, to love me. I am thankful just to know you, to have you in my life, and for letting me be a part of yours. I am thankful that you forced me to let you come here with me this weekend. I am grateful for your ability and willingness to keep me safe, for letting me in, and for showing me that it is okay not to hide anymore. I am thankful that we can laugh so easily together. And I am thankful that the three most incredible people I know, now all know each other. I love you, all of you, and I am thankful for our memories, new and old. I wish this night - this moment - could last forever." Sam lowered her eyes momentarily.

"And Trick?" she grinned as the dog jumped to his feet expectantly at the sound of his name. "I am very thankful that you let me sleep in my bed with you whenever I'm home." Trick panted hopefully as the women laughed. Sam rubbed her fingernails lightly up and down the fur on his back, while Trick leaned against her, still watching the turkey on the table, just in case.

Sarah waited a moment as the laughter died down, then raised her own glass.

"I will keep this brief, I promise!" she smiled, looking at each of them. "I just wanted to say that I am very thankful to be here, with all of you. It has been my true honour to finally meet the women who loved and raised Sam up to be the woman I know and love today. She is my match, it's true, and for that I am eternally grateful. I am thankful for all of you, for welcoming me so openly and so readily into your home, and into your hearts. And I will do everything I can to protect and honour this trust you have placed in me. I am thankful for this meal...which we ALL had a hand in, however small..." she said, faking a glare in Sam's direction, "and I promise that I will make the effort each and every day to be worthy of being an adopted member of this family, as you are all now a part of mine. Thank you, all, and Happy Thanksgiving."

When the clinking of glasses had grown quiet once again, Emily flashed a grin, the candlelight glinting playfully in her blue eyes. She winked at Trick, then turned to the others.

"Well said, everyone, that was very...overwhelming. And wonderful. Now, let's see if this meal worked out to be deserving of all the praise we've just lavished upon it! Dig in!"

The four women immediately began to fill their plates, helping themselves to the vast array of food that they'd busily prepared all afternoon long, while cheerful chatter and lighthearted laughter once again filled the evening air.

*   *   *

"So Em," Samantha said around a mouthful of turkey stuffing. She loved Julie's stuffing almost more than anything. It was just like Mom used to make. *Or so they tell me*, she smiled to herself. "So, are you gonna date that cop guy, or what?" Sam grinned impishly at the shocked expression on her sister's face. She loved finally having something to tease Emily about, rather than the other way around, almost as much as she loved Julie's stuffing. She raised her eyebrows inquisitively, as all eyes at the table turned to see how Emily would respond. Emily finished chewing what was in her mouth and swallowed, attempting to regain her composure while she crafted a suitable reply.

"As a matter of fact," she answered, somewhat slyly, "Ryan has asked me to accompany him to dinner on Friday evening, and I have accepted." It was Samantha's turn to be shocked.

"What?! Really?!" she squealed excitedly. "That's amazing!" Sam shook her head in wonder as Emily laughed, nodding her head in affirmation. "But how...I mean..." Sam turned to look at Julie, who was gazing steadily at Emily, a strange look upon her face. "Like, Jules, did you know about this? I mean, did you have any idea?" Julie shook her head slowly, still looking at Emily.

"Not exactly," she muttered quietly. Sarah met Sam's questioning look with a shrug, so she turned her attention back to Emily, who was now blushing from more than just the wine.

"So, how did all of this happen, exactly? And *when*? I'm assuming he asked you at the farm today, but...like...it's a little weird that he would recognize you after all these years, isn't it? I mean, it's great, and all...you must have made one hell of an impression back then, as of course, you would...but...it's still a little weird, isn't it? In a good way, though?" Sam watched, somewhat confused, as Emily lowered her fork to her plate, and dabbed at her lips with a napkin. She held her breath as Emily took a sip from her wine glass, and folded her hands in front of her, looking briefly at each of them before she spoke.

"Actually, I suppose there is something I should tell you," Emily began, "and I think it's something I probably should have told you a long time ago. I just didn't know how at the time, and eventually, I guess I managed to convince myself that it was better not to, so I just always...kept it to myself." Samantha looked at Julie, then returned her gaze to Emily.

"So...what is it?" she asked. "Have you been seeing this guy behind our backs all this time, or something?" She'd meant it as a joke, trying to crack the sudden tension, but instead of laughing, Emily only sighed, lowering her eyes to her lap.

"Something like that," she quietly replied. Sam sat back in her chair, waiting, along with the others, for her sister to explain. She seemed suddenly nervous, which was rather uncharacteristic for Emily. She took a deep breath, and plunged in.

"I don't want you to be angry," she began, "either of you." She glanced at Julie, then back into her lap again. "I just never knew how to tell you." She sighed. "Officer Mullen ... Ryan ... recognized me today at the farm because...because we've seen each other more recently than just 25 years ago. More recently, and more often." Emily met her sisters' confused stares evenly, inhaled again, and continued. "We've seen each other a lot over the years, I suppose...I guess because I couldn't let go." Everyone at the table fell silent. Even Trick was sitting patiently, watching attentively, seeming to also be waiting for Emily to explain herself.

"Samie, you may have been too young to remember, but Jules, you know...Ryan came by the house a lot after that first night, to check in on us, and he kept us up-to-date on the investigation, right from its earliest stages. He even came to every court appearance made during the trial...remember?" Julie and Samantha both nodded, encouraging her to go on.

"The thing of it was...and this is what I should have told you at the time, I know...is that I couldn't let it go. I was researching everything I could find about the man who'd killed our parents, reading every newspaper article, every interview. I became kind of obsessed, I guess," she admitted sheepishly. "I needed to know, as much as I could, about the man who had done this terrible thing. The man who had taken so much from us." Emily looked at them all, pleadingly.

"Even after his conviction and sentencing, I wasn't done. I couldn't stop. I...I convinced Ryan to let me know each and every time he was up for parole, every appeal, every hearing...every time that man left his *cell*, I wanted to know about it." Emily gazed unseeing at the plate in front of her, lost in memories. "And then I...I got Ryan to take me to court with him, so I could sit in the back and watch as the man who'd stolen our lives pleaded with the court to restore his. I wanted him to see my face, and every single time, know that there was at least one person in the world who knew exactly what he had done. I wanted him to know that, no matter the outcome of any of those hearings, in that one act at least, he was *not* forgiven. I wanted him to know that there was no pardon coming to him. I wanted him to have a visual reminder that, for the rest of his life, the guilt of what he'd done that night would follow him, as the pain of it follows us. I wanted to make sure that he never forgot a single moment of it, even now that his sentence has been served, and he's been released." Sam stared at her, mouth falling open in disbelief.

"He was released?!" she asked, incredulous. "When?"

"Yesterday." Julie's quiet voice filled the room, and everyone around the table caught their breath. She'd been staring at Emily silently the entire time, but now her gaze broke and fell instead to the nearly untouched plate of food in front of her. The already-palpable tension between the two sisters increased. "You're right," she said to Emily in a low voice. "You should have told us."

"I know," Emily sighed. "I'm sorry. I was afraid. Afraid of how you would react...especially when..." She took another deep breath and closed her eyes. "When you found out that yesterday wasn't the first time I'd gone to see him."

A silence fell over the room. No one dared to breathe. Emily finally heaved a tired sigh and quietly sobbed once before continuing.

"I needed to hear, from him, what really happened that night. I...I couldn't let go until I knew." Julie fixed Emily with an icy gaze, while Sam and Sarah watched in silent fear of whatever was coming next. Julie's voice was barely above a whisper.

"And did he tell you?" Julie didn't even blink as Emily nodded slowly. "What did he say?"

Emily looked up then, tears streaming down her face as she

regarded each of them in turn.

"It's...horrible," she stated quietly. "More horrible than you can imagine. But, I realize now, you have a right to know, both of you." She paused, wiping her eyes with a napkin, coughed once, and inhaled deeply once more. Then, without looking up, she relayed the entire mortifying story almost exactly as Duncan Rolston had told it to her so many years ago.

~9~

Duncan realized that Emily Collins would know most of the story already - from a clinical, distant perspective, at any rate. The trial and headlines alone would have told the general order of events as they had occurred. Now, however, Duncan had intended to give her more of the details than she'd ever really wanted to hear. She had, after all, asked for it.

Duncan Rolston, then twenty-five years of age, had gone with his friends, Tobias "Toby" Walden and Randall "Rand" Mellinkoff, to pay their dealer a visit prior to heading to a Halloween party they'd been planning to attend. The men had met said dealer (who had somehow managed to remain anonymous throughout the entire course of the investigation - Duncan had heard that the cowardly bastard had skipped town upon hearing of his pending arrest) under a bridge near the park on the city's east side. Under the cover of darkness, they had all done a couple of speedballs, and had then parted ways. The young men had decided to take a walk across the park before going anywhere, as it had been an unusually pleasant evening out, and none of them had felt like being indoors right away.

They had all three been talking and laughing; the park oddly deserted for that time of evening, and had stopped to stand and have a smoke near one of the old cast iron benches that spotted park the area along the worn pathways. That was when the conversation between the three friends had taken what would end up being a fatal turn. There they had stood, boastfully embellishing on their most recent sexual conquests as though they'd been standing in a locker room after winning the big game, and Rand had suddenly let it slip that he'd managed to score a makeout session at a bar with Duncan's then-drunken girlfriend, Ashleigh, less than a week prior to that night's events. Well, Duncan silently admitted to himself, Ashleigh hadn't actually and fully been his girlfriend, per se, but at the time, the details hadn't mattered. Duncan had stared at his friend, a sudden silence falling over the park. Smoke curled around his head as he'd exhaled - and then exploded in a billowing fury as Duncan had punched Rand square in the jaw. Rand had staggered back, momentarily off balance and, seeing red, Duncan had pursued, relentless. Rand had blocked his next swing, and Duncan had been vaguely aware of Toby trying to break in and separate them, when Duncan had grabbed Rand by the shoulders and slammed him, hard, against a nearby tree.

There had been a sickening crunch, and Rand had suddenly gone rigid, grunted once, and then stared off vacantly into space, his last breath coming out in a quiet choked off sigh. A branch had long ago been broken off the trunk of the tree, leaving behind just enough of a stump to easily pierce the back of Rand's skull when his head had hit upon it. It had remained lodged in his brain and became a kind of bizarre coat hangar when Duncan had released his grip on him; Rand's body dangling from the stump like a strange stringless marionette.

Randall Mellinkoff was dead.

"Oh my God..." Toby had whispered into the sudden stillness of the night. It was the last time Duncan and Toby would agree on anything.

*   *   *

The events immediately following Rand's death (*Murder*, Duncan reminded himself. *I was angry and I killed him. It was murder.*) were largely a blur in Duncan's drug-addled mind. He had resisted the urge to just cut and run, and instead quickly formulated a plan of action. Duncan Rolston, the fourth generation in a line of powerful self-made multi-millionaires, stood on the verge of not only inheriting his family's fortune, but was well on his way to adding to it impressively himself. In other words, Duncan Rolston *was* a man of action.

He remembered pulling Rand's body off the now sticky and bloody broken branch stump, and dropping him to the ground. Dimly, he recalled his disgust at the sound it had made, as the tree released its death grip on Rand's punctured skull, and his further disgust when he realized Toby was vomiting violently into a nearby bush. Wiping absently at his mouth when he'd finished, Toby staggered toward Duncan, shock and fear plastered across his face. Duncan watched him silently for a moment, then assumed an expression of calm but unmistakable authority. He gestured casually at the lifeless body now staining the dirt with blood.

"Search his pockets," he commanded in a low voice. "Get his wallet, and his car keys. His watch. Anything of value." Toby had gaped at him blankly.

"W-what?" he'd stammered, shaking his head in disbelief. "Dunc - dude...we have to call the *cops*, man, not..." Duncan had cut him off with a wave of his hand, and had explained, in no uncertain terms, what the repercussions of that particular course of action would be. Blubbering quietly to himself, Toby had finally relented, and had bent to his grisly task while Duncan lit another cigarette and surveyed the surrounding park. No one had seen anything yet, he was certain. But they would have to move quickly to ensure that it stayed that way.

His grisly task at last accomplished, Toby had straightened and stared at Duncan, wiping sweat from his ashen face as he awaited further instruction. Duncan had nodded in satisfaction.

"Let's go," he muttered. "We don't have much time."

The two had walked briskly across the darkened park, trying to move quickly without appearing to be in a rush. They hadn't wanted to draw attention to themselves. They had reached Rand's truck, a sleek black Dodge Ram, within a few minutes, but to Duncan, it seemed as though hours had passed. He hadn't wanted to glance over his shoulder, lest it appear as though he were running from something, but with every precious step he put between himself and Rand's body, he'd held his breath, expecting at any moment to hear someone sound an alarm once the body was discovered. He stalked purposefully to the driver's side, and gestured at Toby to get in the passenger seat, raising a warning finger before Toby could protest that they were in no shape to drive. Duncan was fairly certain that the events of the past 10 minutes had sobered him up completely. Shivering, he set his jaw, put the vehicle in drive, and sped off into the night.

*   *   *

Duncan hadn't even seen the end of the road approaching. He'd been yelling at Toby, trying to calm him down so that he could concentrate. They'd driven out of the city limits; Duncan planning to ditch the truck to make the robbery scenario all the more complete. He'd felt they could still make an appearance at the party, even, and no one would be the wiser. To Duncan, it had seemed the perfect plan. Internally, he'd been near-congratulatory, feeling both pleased and powerful with having just gotten away with a terrible, but in his mind unavoidable, mistake. If only he'd been able to think more clearly, without Toby panicking loudly in the seat beside him. Keeping one hand on the steering wheel, he had reached over with the other and thrust Toby's head against the passenger side window, screaming at him to shut the hell up. Toby had fought back, lashing out in fear and anger, and had managed to land a lucky punch squarely on Duncan's jaw. His head had flipped to the side and he'd shut his eyes briefly against the explosion of pain inside his head.

That was all it had taken.

Duncan and Toby's vehicle had flown past a stop sign and into the partial intersection, where they would have ended up harmlessly crashing through a small wire fence into an empty field - had it not been for one lone vehicle coursing along the open highway through that same intersection, at that same moment. In an instant, the whole world seemed to shriek and burst apart in an unearthly cry of squealing tires and twisting steel. Duncan felt himself hurled forward as his seatbelt snapped into its locked position, and then abruptly jerked back, his neck popping in agony, as the airbags inside the vehicle were deployed. Barely aware of the sudden silence, Duncan slumped in his seat, and passed out.

*   *   *

As he regained consciousness, Duncan groaned, and rubbed his neck. He had been fairly certain that he'd have a wicked case of whiplash to contend with, on top of everything else. Like a nightmare, the evenings events had washed over him in a wave of terror and nausea, and before his eyes were even open, Duncan had fumbled for the door handle while tugging off his seatbelt, and tumbled out of the truck, vomiting onto the cold pavement below. Gasping gratefully as fresh air filled his lungs, Duncan had staggered to his feet, and looked around. *What the fuck did I hit?* he had wondered, squinting into the darkness surrounding him. A moment later, he had seen his answer.

Or, rather, he had heard it.

"Help!"

The cry came faint but clear from somewhere nearby. Rounding the front of the truck - Rand's truck - Duncan came startled upon yet another horrific scene from this nightmare evening. Another vehicle...a car...was lodged partway into a ditch on the other side of the road. It had been smashed nearly in two yet, miraculously, at least one occupant was still alive. Duncan could see a man - the source of the voice he'd heard - struggling to free himself from the wreckage. He was leaning across a woman, unconscious, on the passenger side, pounding on the crumpled car door, trying to get Duncan's attention. Their eyes locked. The man's frantic blue gaze turned desperate; pleading.

"Please," he cried. "My wife, she's hurt! I can't get her out!" He renewed his futile pounding on the door handle with increased energy. "The car..." The man gestured toward the shattered front end of his vehicle, and Duncan's mind snapped to full alert when he saw the issue to which the man was referring. The car was on fire. And due to the devastation of the front end, both passengers were trapped in the crumpled wreckage, and the flames were licking ever closer to the vehicle's gas tank. Their car was about to explode.

Duncan stared at the man trapped inside, and froze. The woman had begun to stir, momentarily catching the man's attention. Duncan watched as he kissed his wife's blood-streaked forehead, and tenderly brushed her matted hair from her face. He felt a tear slip down his own cheek as the man looked back at him, their eyes meeting for a second, and final time.

Please...help us... The man's mouth moved but no sound came out. Just then, the night erupted in an explosion of sound and a blinding flash of light. Duncan felt the concussion under his feet even as the force of the eruption pushed him onto his back; his ears ringing violently. Clutching his head, Duncan scrambled to his knees and gaped in horror at the burning wreckage; the people trapped inside now incinerated before his eyes.

"No..." Duncan whispered, his mind reeling. He staggered to his feet, and stumbled against Rand's truck, holding himself upright by leaning awkwardly on the hood.

"Dude..." Toby's voice seemed to come from right beside him, and from far away, at the same time. Duncan spun around. Toby was awake, and staring at the fiery scene before him. He had a gash on his forehead that was trickling blood, unbeknownst to Toby, down the side of his face and dripping onto his shoulder. Without thinking, Duncan stalked to the truck door, pulled it open, and yanked on Toby's jacket.

"Out," he commanded. "We have got to go. *Now.*" Toby stared a moment longer, looking from Duncan to the burning vehicle and back again, in growing confusion and terror.

"What happened?" he croaked. "I - I don't..." Duncan cut him off by grabbing the collar of his jacket with both hands and pulling Toby forward until their faces were mere inches apart.

"Listen to me!" he yelled hoarsely. "We have got to go! Right now! Ask questions later. For now, you *RUN!*" And with that, Duncan dropped his arms, turned, and ran back down the road from which they'd just come. Toby stared after him a moment, then jumped from the truck, and followed Duncan as quickly as he could into the still dark night.

*   *   *

Duncan had sat back in his chair when he was finished talking and rubbed absently at his eyes. He was suddenly exhausted, and had an incredible headache. But overall, he thought he felt better - lighter - than

108

he had at any point since that one regrettable night. He stretched and looked back at the photograph on the table. The faces smiling out at him now seemed almost forgiving; accepting, even, and they no longer arrested his attention as they had before he'd finally told his side of the story. Duncan Rolston really did feel much better. *And the truth actually shall set you free*, he thought, smiling to himself.

"You son of a bitch." Emily Collins' words snapped him from his reverie, and his eyes flicked up to meet hers. Tears were streaming down her face and she was staring at him, a mix of horror and hatred twisting her features. Duncan searched his mind quickly for an appropriate response; hopefully one that would calm her down before she exploded.

"I'm sorry," he croaked weakly. Emily blinked at him.

"*Sorry?!*" she screamed suddenly. "You're *sorry?!*" She jumped to her feet, her chair clattering loudly to the floor.

Too late, he thought, backpeddaling. "I mean - I'm...um..."

"FUCK YOU!" she shrieked, leaping at him, as officers ran toward them. "They were *alive!*" she cried. "They were alive and you *killed them!*" Then she was on him, slapping at him and screaming into his face until his ears rang. Duncan brought his arms up to ward off her flailing punches. "*Murderer!*" yelled. "You murdered my parents! You'll *never* get out of here, you bastard! If it's the last thing I do, I'll see you rot in *hell!*"

The officers had her then; Mullen and another one. They hauled her off of him, and began dragging her toward the exit. *Kicking and screaming*, he thought. *Literally.* Duncan ruefully rubbed his jaw where she'd managed to land a sound blow before finally being pulled off of him. He watched, speechless, as Emily Collins was practically carried from the room, the door at last cutting off her hysterical cries as it closed behind her. He glanced back at the table, where her now-forgotten family photograph still lay; the smiling faces seeming less forgiving to him now. Duncan closed his hand over the photo, tucking it into a pocket in his shirt when he was reasonably sure no one was paying him much attention any longer, and got to his feet. Struggling to appear nonchalant, he picked his way carefully to the door; demanding to be escorted back to his cell. He had a lot more to think about than he'd realized.

*   *   *

After seeing Emily Collins and that cop waiting outside the prison gate as he was released, Duncan had sat silently in the dark sedan, watching the scenery go by as the car sped along its way without really seeing any of it. In his mind, he was still lost in the past; a past he wished he could forget, but knew he never would. He'd lost so much because of that one horrible night. That one night, when his mistakes had compounded, one after the other, snowballing out of his control long before he'd ever realized it. And it had cost him. His best friends (he and Toby had not spoken since Toby had testified against him to save his own skin; and Rand, of course, was still as dead as ever), his education, his fortune, and his entire future. Even his family, though they'd stood by him publicly, had never looked at him the same way again. He felt a nervous knot in his stomach swell at the notion of returning to his parents' lavish home after all this time locked away from the outside world, but he knew he had nowhere else to go, and had resigned himself to it long ago. It seemed odd to him, and frightening, to be starting a new life so late in life. However, there really was nothing left of the old one. He couldn't just go pick up where he'd left off, after all. He would have to find a new way, by starting all over again from the beginning. Yes, Duncan Rolston really had lost everything over the course of that one horrific night.

But he knew now that what he had taken - from Rand, the Mellinkoffs, and from the whole Collins family - had been so much more. Officially, Duncan had paid his debt to society in full, with the service of his entire prison term. However, the debt he owed to the lives he'd ruined had not even a dent. Duncan knew that one would never be repaid; that it couldn't be repaid. It simply wasn't possible. And with that realization weighing heavily on his heart, Duncan Rolston knew, unequivocally, that particular debt, along with the now worn and faded photograph he still kept in his pocket, would be the only thing from his old life that he'd carry forward, into his new one.

*   *   *

110

Emily continued to stare at her hands on the table when she had finished telling her sisters of the terrible secret she had been carrying for so long. She realized that she didn't feel even a little bit better for the unburdening.

"I'm so sorry I didn't tell you before," she whispered sadly. "I didn't think..."

"No you DIDN'T think!" Julie exploded suddenly. "How could you keep something like that from us?!" she cried. "How could you keep it from *me*?" Sam looked helplessly from one sister to the other, tears in her eyes. She felt sick to her stomach. Even on top of everything that had just been revealed to her, Sam hated when her sisters fought, more than anything. It was the worst feeling in the world, and she suddenly felt very small and confused.

"But I don't understand," she broke in weakly. "Yesterday..." She caught her breath as Julie rounded on her.

"Yesterday," she fumed, "*yesterday* he was *released*. He's served his full sentence. And you were *there*!" Julie was furious. "You were *there*, you *saw* him. Yesterday! You've been there before! You've even *spoken* to him! You've known the whole sickening truth about what happened to our parents all this time! And all this time, all these years, you never said *one...single...word*." Julie pounded her fist on the table, punctuating each word.

"I...I didn't want..." Emily stopped, waving one hand in the air in front of her face, as if erasing what she had just been about to say. She started again. "It was something I needed to do, for *me*," she explained, a tear trickling down her cheek. "If either of you had asked, or shown more than a passing interest in what happened to him after sentencing, I would have brought you along, or at least kept you filled in. But it wasn't...you were able to move on without knowing all of that. You were able to heal and go on with your lives. I...was not. And it was horrible. So, so horrible, knowing what had really happened...that they'd actually still..." she choked. "I thought if I could spare you that much, at least, then maybe...maybe..." Emily broke down then, her head in her hands. No one spoke. Sarah had reached over and taken Samantha's hand, and gave it a gentle squeeze of support and Sam sat staring at her sisters, tears streaming silently down her face.

"I'm not sorry I did it," Emily whispered, sniffling. "But I am sorry...very sorry...that I didn't tell you." She raised her head and her eyes fell on Julie's own tear-stained face. "Please," she whispered. "I'm so sorry, Jules." Julie pushed her chair back and stood, stepping over to hug Emily tightly.

"I love you, Em," she said quietly, returning to her seat. "I just don't understand why you would keep something like that from me. Something so big; so important. I feel like you...didn't trust me, or something." Her voice trailed off, seemingly unsure if she'd be able to get her point across without escalating the conversation back into an argument again. Emily wiped at her eyes, then fixed Julie with a steady, unwavering gaze.

"I think you know very well how I could feel the need to keep something like that to myself," she said firmly. "To spare the rest of you from the burden of knowing a terrible truth. After all, there's something pretty huge and important that you haven't exactly been completely forthcoming with, as well, isn't there?" Julie blanched visibly.

"What...?" Filled with an icy dread, and suddenly unable to speak, Julie gaped, open-mouthed, at her sister. Emily didn't back down. She merely took another sip of wine, and set down her glass, her eyes never leaving Julie's face.

"There's a secret you've been carrying around, mostly alone, for too long now. And I think it's time you let it out, too."

*   *   *

Julie couldn't breathe. She couldn't think. All she could do was stare in confused horror at her sister. *How could she know?* Julie wondered frantically. She thought to glance at Sarah, to see if she could tell whether the woman had said anything, or not, but she refrained. Sarah didn't seem the type, and besides, she didn't really know anything. Julie nervously licked her lips, considering. Emily seemed fairly certain of something so, whatever she was referring to was likely something that Julie already knew that she knew. Unable to come up with any other response, Julie opted to play dumb.

112

"I'm not sure I know what you're talking about," she replied simply. Emily nodded slightly, as though she'd expected as much, but that Julie had still just managed to disappoint her, regardless.

"You're not, huh?" Emily met her stare. "Well, let me refresh your memory a little. There's something you haven't said much to me about, and that you haven't told Samantha about at all." Emily paused, then fixed Julie with a pointed look. "About why you're *here*," she said. "About why you moved back home when you did." Sudden realization dawned on Julie, and she exhaled slowly in relief mixed with mild trepidation. She'd continued staring at Emily, but she had noticed Sam's head turn swiftly in her direction as soon as Emily had mentioned their youngest sister's name. She couldn't believe she was about to have this conversation, after all. She sighed, her eyes dropping to the table as she tried to decide where to start.

"Okay, Em," she said in resignation. "Okay." Julie raised her head and looked at each woman apologetically. "She's right," she said. "I've been keeping something mostly to myself, for a few years now. Emily only knows what she knows because I asked her to come and get me. But I guess it really is time that I come clean about the rest of it." Julie took a single shaky breath, and then spoke quickly, not wanting to relive the memory, but attempting instead to get it all out as painlessly as possible.

"It's about Richard," she began. "My ex-husband," she added as an afterthought, for Sarah's sake. "Basically, well...he was a good enough guy, most of the time, you know? Worked hard, and all that. But he had a real mean streak to him - a kind of rage - and it seemed to get worse and worse as time went on. We started off just having really bad arguments sometimes, but...but then he started throwing things, breaking things...punching walls. That sort of thing." Julie glanced quickly at Sam, and the expression she saw on her sister's face nearly broke her heart. It seemed as though she could tell where this was going already. *At least this part of it*, Julie thought sadly.

"I guess, really, it was only a matter of time before he turned all that rage onto me," she stated into the ensuing silence.

"What did he do?" It was Sarah who had whispered the question, but Julie knew she was speaking on everyone's behalf, encouraging her to

113

continue. She wiped a tear away as she took a breath, and continued.

"He hit me," she said simply. "But it was more than that, really. It was like he was trying to break me, in every way he could think of. He'd destroy things if he thought they meant something to me, or keep them from me until he felt I'd suitably apologized for whatever he thought I'd done to wrong him that day. He'd show up, drunk, at three o'clock in the morning, and be angry if I was in bed, instead of waiting up for him. Or, if I waited up, he was angry that I hadn't gone to bed, thinking that meant that I didn't trust him, and that I was waiting up to spy on him, or something." Julie paused, taking another shaky breath. "It got so that he...was just always angry. And always with me. He'd say...horrible things to me...the kind of things you never forget, but that you never want to hear spoken aloud again, you know?" Everyone at the table nodded in understanding and sympathy, though Julie didn't seem to notice. She was staring at her hands, lost in thought.

"Then one night...that night," she said slowly, glancing at Emily, "that night, he came home early, angrier than I'd ever seen him. I'd made dinner but hadn't set it on the table by the time he'd walked in, and...I don't know...he just seemed to lose it. He destroyed the kitchen, everything I'd just made..." Julie coughed, unable to slow the tears flowing from her eyes. "He backhanded me, only once, but it was hard enough to knock me into the edge of the table and onto the floor. I couldn't catch my breath, at first, and then all of a sudden he was on me, kicking me over and over and over. He wouldn't stop. He just wouldn't stop." Julie was sobbing at the memory, but was determined to continue, to get it all out, once and for all.

"After that...something about it...I guess something got him even more worked up. I could hear him breathing really heavy, as he was standing over me. And then I heard him undo his belt. I still couldn't breathe, and I was crying and trying to scream, but the sound wouldn't come out. I didn't know how to stop him." Julie whimpered, ashamed, through the sobs now racking her body. *Just a little bit more*, she thought to herself. *You're almost there.* She could hear her sisters crying alongside of her, but continued to stare at her hands. She needed to finish this before she lost her nerve.

"I guess the neighbours heard some of what was going on," she continued in a low voice. "And they had called the police. They arrived just in time to...stop him...for the most part. And they took him away. An ambulance came and took me to the hospital. I was bleeding a lot, I guess, and apparently I blacked out for awhile on the way over. When I woke up, a nurse told me that they'd called Emily, and that she was on her way there, to be with me. The doctor came in to talk to me, first, before you arrived." Julie glanced briefly at Emily but, unable to stand the anguish she saw on her sister's face, returned her gaze to her hands once again. "The doctor...he told me...a few th-things.." Julie was on the verge of tears again, but took a deep breath and managed to keep herself from losing control. "He told me that I was going to be okay, first off. But he told me that I would have to stay overnight, for observation. Richard had done some real damage, apparently, and they wanted to keep an eye on me, just to be sure. He'd broken some ribs, and bruised my back so badly that they were unable to tell if there was any internal damage until after some of the swelling had gone down. And finally," Julie paused, not wanting to speak the next words out loud, but knowing that she had to, if she was ever going to be able to let it all go. "The last thing he told me, was something I never shared, even with you, Em. Until now." She paused again, then closed her eyes, and forged ahead. "There'd been a...I was...I'd lost..." Julie stammered, struggling to get the words out. "I'd been pregnant," she breathed. Sam cried out in shock and despair; Sarah covered her mouth with one hand, while she held tight to Samantha with the other. Emily sat still as a stone, tears of mortification falling silently from her eyes.

"Jules," she whispered, but stopped as Julie waved a hand in the air to cut her off.

"It had only been a few weeks," she said, as though that made a difference. "I didn't even know myself, until...until the doctor told me...he told me." Julie covered her face and sobbed once, then straightened, trying in vain to regain her composure. She looked at her sisters, wide-eyed, like a panicked child desperately seeking the answer they wanted to hear, whether it was true, or not.

"I mean...I can't lose what I never knew I had...right?" She looked at them as Emily stood up, Sam and Sarah following suit, and shook her head, watching as they all moved slowly toward her. "No," she cried. "I didn't know! I didn't know, so I couldn't have..." With a convulsive wail,

Julie fell into her sisters' arms, clinging to them as she at last gave into her overwhelming grief.

"I'm so sorry, sweetie," Emily whispered over and over, holding her tightly until her tears slowed and were spent. "I'm so sorry."

*   *   *

Emily sat curled up in the huge armchair in a corner of the living room, flipping through an old magazine, and trying to relax her swirling mind. An exhausted Trick was sprawled out, snoring, in front of the fireplace, which was crackling contentedly; its warmth spreading slowly throughout the house, and beating back the chill of the late October night. Candles and subdued lamps had replaced the overhead lights, while soft music played unobtrusively in the background. She felt as though half her lifetime had passed since yesterday morning. And yet it seemed impossible that Sam and Sarah would be leaving the next day. It still felt to Emily, despite everything that had transpired, as though they had just arrived. All things being equal, though, it also seemed impossible that she'd really only known Sarah for not quite two days. Time was a funny thing, when you thought about it, Emily decided.

She turned the page in her magazine, no longer even seeing the words, so much as she was just glancing at the pictures. The girls had all held onto Julie, after her horrible revelation, until she'd stopped crying enough that she was able to climb back into her chair. Sarah had quietly cleared the rest of the meal away, packaging it up and miraculously finding room in the over-stuffed refrigerator to store it all for the next day. Sam had carefully walked Julie upstairs to her room, as her strength had still seemed too precarious to make it completely under her own steam, while Emily had gotten started on cleaning the dishes. No one had spoken, except in very low voices and only very briefly, at most. Sarah had appeared to help Emily finish the dishes, and then had gone upstairs looking for Samantha. Emily had gotten changed into more comfortable clothes, after checking to make sure that everyone was more or less taken care of and, not knowing what else to do with her restless energy, had poured herself another healthy glass of wine, and settled into the living room for awhile.

The house was quiet around her. She flipped another page, then

116

looked up as Trick lifted his head, blinking away sleep, and staring lazily off in the direction of the stairs. With a sigh, he heaved himself to his feet, and padded softly over to the foot of the stairs, tail wagging loosely while he slowly worked to wake himself up. Moments later, Samantha and Sarah appeared in the doorway, both also seemingly unsure as to what to do with the rest of their evening. Emily closed her magazine, and tossed it onto the newspaper pile in the corner behind her chair.

"Hey," Sam said quietly. "I was wondering...if you know where it is, I mean...I was wondering if maybe I could show the Halloween album to Sarah?" She scratched the back of her head absently, still standing rather uncomfortably just inside the door. "Just to, you know, prepare her..." Sam frowned, and shook her head. "I just...the ones we were showing her were mostly pictures of just us, you know? That one, though, has more of Mom and Dad, too, and I thought..." her voice trailed off uncertainly.

"I think that's a wonderful idea," Emily smiled. "I've been meaning to pull it out and get it ready so that we can add to it this year, too. Let me see..." Emily got up and went to the large bookcase that took up the entire back wall of the living room area. Aside from a framed picture or treasured knick-knack here and there, the entire case was almost completely packed full of books. There were novels, in both hard and soft covers, old textbooks from school that the girls didn't want to get rid of, for whatever reason, and even an entire, albeit beat up and dusty, old set of encyclopedia, which their parents had bought in separate volumes after Emily was born. And there were photos...most in albums, but some just in old shoeboxes, still waiting for someone to find the time to put them away properly. Emily crouched in front of the stuffed bookcase, searching for one well-used album in particular. She knew it wouldn't be very difficult to find.

"Here we go," she said, standing up and holding the album out in her hand. Sarah stared at it a moment, and then her face broke into a grin. Sam and Emily smiled, too, watching her reaction. The infamous Collins Halloween Photo Album was now a treasured family heirloom and was, even after all these years, still quite a sight to behold. Emily couldn't even remember when her father had first created it for their mother. *In fact*, she thought, *this may even have been around before I was!* What had once started long ago as a cute holiday project, however, had grown into something even its creator couldn't have predicted.

Two pieces of thick, sturdy cardboard had been cut in the shape of a pumpkin, and covered with a bright orange cloth, to resist fading. He'd decorated the cloth, using a black permanent marker, to look like the front and back of a Jack-o'-Lantern, and had fastened both parts together using some brown yarn. The pages inside contained pictures and notes from each year at Halloween, from the album's inception all the way up to and including a few from the year before. The girls had all agreed to keep it going even after the accident but, while all three sisters had occasionally contributed, the book really had turned more into Emily's pet project over the years. She ran one hand fondly over the cover, smiling to herself.

"Could you help?" Samantha asked suddenly, breaking into her reverie. She blushed slightly as Emily looked up at her quizzically. "I just...your memory is so much better than mine," she explained. "And...I kinda like hearing you tell the stories. Could you? Just for a little while?" Sam begged. Before Emily could answer, a third figure appeared in the doorway behind the girls.

"What am I missing?" Julie asked, a shy smile on her lips. Sam grinned at her.

"Em's gonna help me show Sarah the Halloween album!" she enthused with her particular brand of child-like glee, then took Julie gently by the hand. "We sure could use your input, too, Jules. If you wouldn't mind?" Julie glanced at Emily, and a brief private look passed between them. They were okay. Then Julie smiled, squeezed her younger sister's hand, and took Sarah's arm, pulling them both over to the couch.

"Absolutely,' Julie grinned. "Em gets some of the stories wrong, if I don't help!"

"Hey!" Emily tried to appear insulted, but at Sam's happy giggle, she gave up and cracked a conniving smile of her own. "Whatever, Jules," she laughed. "Maybe if you're good, I'll let you at least turn the pages, this time!" Emily managed to duck out of the way just as Julie turfed a pillow at her, and it sailed harmlessly over her head. "You're lucky I am unarmed, little sister," Emily warned her with a wink. At that, all four women dissolved into a fit of giggles, piling onto the couch together as

Emily worked to undo the knot keeping the book closed.

When everyone had quieted down and she was ready to begin, she opened the worn cover, and spread her hand gently over the first faded page of photos. They featured their mother, young, beautiful, and very very pregnant with their first child. Apparently their parents had thought it hilarious to paint a giant Jack-o'-Lantern face onto her huge swollen belly, and they'd taken several pictures of it...their father taking a self-portrait with the pumpkin belly; the pumpkin belly wearing a hat; the pumpkin belly balancing a bowl of goodies on its 'head', ready to hand out to all of the little trick-or-treaters that would be arriving at their door. Both of their parents looked so young, happy and in love. Emily smiled down at their beautiful, faded faces, and began the tale of the Collins' Halloween Legacy.

"In the beginning," she said solemnly, pointing at her mother's pregnant pumpkin, "there was me." The room erupted in laughter again, and Emily grinned at the beautiful faces surrounding her in the firelight, relieved and thankful to have the house feeling warm and happy once more.

*   *   *

Julie felt awful. Every cell in her body seemed to be screaming in pain and exhaustion. As a result, she'd agreed to let Emily drive Samantha and Sarah back to the airport, but had insisted on going along for the ride. She hadn't gotten much in the way of actual sleep over the weekend, but she was determined not to miss any more of the time she had with her sister and Sarah. She wanted to squeeze every last minute out of it, regardless of how tired she may be feeling sometimes.

As the car sped toward the airport, Julie reflected upon how different this trip was from the one that they had taken back to the house when she'd picked the girls up just a few days before. So much had happened in the time in between, and now they were all four together, and all, she suspected, much closer now than they had been mere days ago. Julie wondered if it was somehow Sarah's calm influence; if that had somehow allowed the sisters to drop their guard somewhat, or if it had perhaps been a sort of snowball effect. She glanced at Sam's reflection in the rearview mirror. Her sister was once again riding in the back seat, this time with Sarah at her side, since Julie was now riding shotgun. Sam had bolted from the house that first night, and though Julie still did not know what had precipitated that incident, she felt that it had somehow been the catalyst required to set all of the other events that had happened into motion. Julie made a mental note to one day find out just what it was that had sent Sam running from the house a second time. She suspected that both instances were somehow linked, and that finding out what had caused one would also give her the reason behind the other. After all that had happened over the weekend, Julie was more certain than ever that her youngest sibling was carrying something secret around inside of her, and that it was something she and Emily had never even come close to guessing at. Julie had no idea what it could be, but she was now all the more determined to find out. For Samantha's sake, more than anything else.

She turned her attention to the conversation now taking place. Emily was asking something about how they would get back to their apartment after they landed.

"Oh, our friend, Andre will be picking us up," Sarah replied, glancing quickly at Sam. Samantha's head snapped around to stare at her.

"What?" she asked, suddenly irritated. "We don't need a ride. We left the car at the airport..."

"We did," Sarah responded defensively, "but I called to let him know we were leaving town, after all, and he offered to retrieve the car and pick us up today."

"You cal- *really*?!" Sam rolled her eyes in disgust. "Well, that's just fan*tas*tic, Sarah. Truly. That makes my whole *day*!"

"He *offered*," Sarah repeated firmly, seeming irritated herself, now. "I thought it was nice. Generous of him, really, considering." Sam rolled her eyes again and glared out the window.

"Whatever," she muttered under her breath. Emily glanced at Julie, then back into the girls' reflection in the mirror.

"Okay, who's Andre?" she asked, clearly wanting to get to the bottom of whatever was bothering her sister and Sarah before they went much further.

"He's a friend of mine," Sarah explained. "We had a couple of theatre classes together a few years ago..."

"And they used to date," Sam cut in angrily. "And now he's stalking her, trying to get her back. He's pathetic. He keeps hanging around, trying to keep us from spending any time alone together. But meanwhile he'll ask her to go do all this stuff with him, and completely ignore the fact that I exist at all."

"That's not true," Sarah retorted. "He's hurt, but he's accepted that all that will ever be between us is friendship. He's just trying to be a good friend, the only way he knows how." Sam shook her head angrily.

"If you really believe that, you are more easily fooled than I would have thought," she glowered. "It figures that he'd figure out how to weasel his way into this, too. It just fucking figures." Emily glanced at Julie again, and cut Samantha off before she could say anything more.

"Aaaand, I'm sorry I asked." She shook her head and sighed. "If I may," she continued, "I know it's none of my business, but it seems like you ladies have some things to sort out if you're going to make this relationship work." She looked at their reflection again to make sure they were listening, then turned her attention back to the road ahead. "No one can tell you how to be together," she said. "It's something you have to figure out for yourselves. But I will say that, to anyone looking at you, it is so incredibly obvious that you love one another, and that you want very much to be together. I'll even go so far as to say that it seems to me as though you two are *meant* to be together. And something like that doesn't come along every day. So just...think about what you want. And don't screw it up. Okay?" Both girls nodded sullenly in the back seat, but Julie saw Sarah reach over and take Sam's hand again and, while not looking at her, Sam still gave Sarah's hand an answering squeeze, and continued looking out the window. Emily, seeing it, too, relaxed somewhat, and they drove on together in a more comfortable silence the rest of the way.

They soon arrived at the airport and parked the car. Emily and Julie helped the girls carry their luggage to the point where they would see them off. Julie hugged Sarah as Emily and Sam said a quiet goodbye together off to one side. Julie felt that, above all, the relationship between her two sisters had changed and grown the most over the past couple of days. She hoped to see that trend continue as they felt their way through the next several months together, as Julie sensed, with a pang of guilt and sadness, that the two of them were going to need each other more than they ever had before.

"Take good care of our girl," she whispered to Sarah as they lingered within their embrace.

"I will," Sarah promised, before lightly kissing her on the cheek. "And you take care of *you*, okay?" Her blue eyes searched Julie's face with genuine concern. Julie smiled at her ruefully, and nodded. Then she turned to sweep Samantha up in a tight hug.

"That's a good girl you've got there," she said, watching as her words brought a huge grin to her sister's face.

"She'll do," Sam agreed, as Julie chuckled quietly. "I'm worried about you," Sam said suddenly, a slight frown creasing her forehead. Julie waved off her concern nonchalantly.

"Don't be," she said. "I'll be just fine. Now have a safe flight and I'll see you in a couple of weeks." Sam continued to study her thoughtfully, and Julie lowered her eyes. "We'll talk about it later, I promise, okay? For now, though, I'm fine, so you can stop worrying. Alright?" Sam pursed her lips.

"We'll talk about it later," she repeated with a nod, her concern at least momentarily appeased. "Okay." Julie breathed a silent sigh of relief. *I'll tell them after Halloween*, she promised herself. *You let us have this weekend, so I will keep up my end and tell them together after Halloween*. Her bargain with unknown forces struck, Julie turned to link arms with Emily and watched as the girls made their way to the gate, turning to wave back at them before ducking through the doorway and out of sight. Next to her, Emily sighed heavily.

"Well," she said, matter-of-factly, "*that* went smoothly, wouldn't you say?" Julie laughed as they turned and headed back to where they'd parked the car.

"Oh, like *butter*", she agreed. "I'd even go so far as to call it seamless!" Julie smiled as she listened to Emily's laughter, reveling in the simple moment of happiness while it lasted. In the back of her mind, a tiny, angry voice whispered something about how she would soon be changing all of their lives forever, but Julie thrust that voice aside. *Not yet,* she thought. *Soon, yes, but not yet.*

Walking back to the car, next to Emily, feeling exhausted and yet elevated from the events of the past two days, Julie had the sense that, despite everything, she was feeling lighter in that moment with her sister than she had in years. She clung to that feeling, determined to grab hold and hang onto it for as long as she possibly could. She climbed into the passenger seat and lay her head back on the headrest as Emily started the car. Julie knew such moments would soon become few and far between, and she filed this one away to be called upon again when she needed it. And she would need it, she knew. She glanced at the blue sky overhead, once again feeling at peace in the beautiful autumn weather. She sensed Emily watching her, and turned to smile at her, letting her know, wordlessly, that she was okay, at least for the time being. Emily visibly relaxed, and turned out onto the road which would lead them to the highway; the road that would take them back home.

~10~

Sarah rushed out of the building's far exit doors, pulling her jacket on as she went. She was going to miss the bus, she was sure of it. She was definitely cutting it close, at best. The temperature had dropped and the wind had picked up substantially while she had been in class, and even though it was still fairly early, the sky had already grown dark under the thick carpet of grey clouds skulking overhead. It felt like it could start raining at any moment or, she feared, snowing. Regardless, Sarah very much wanted to be home before any of that mess started.

Her mind preoccupied with making it to the bus loading area in time, Sarah didn't even see the hulking figure step from around the corner of the building she'd been rapidly walking alongside, trying to keep out of the wind, until she'd walked headlong right into it.

"Whoa," she cried. "Oh my God, I am *so sorry*! I wasn't watching and...oh! Andre!" she smiled in relief, recognizing her friend's familiar face. Hands on her shoulders, Andre stepped back, looking her up and down.

"No worries, babe, that was my bad! Almost took you out, there! Sorry!" Satisfied that she was alright, he dropped his arms to his sides, and stood grinning at her.

"What are you doing here?" Sarah asked, returning his smile. He shrugged casually, the wind ruffling his hair.

"Aw, you know," he winked. "I was just in the neighbourhood, and thought I'd see if you wanted to go for dinner, or something. My treat," he added hastily. Sarah sighed regretfully.

"Oh, Andre, that's...incredibly sweet. But I can't tonight, I'm sorry. I - we - have plans this evening. I actually really have to get going..."

"So," he cut her off, "you're just heading home, then, I guess?" Sarah nodded, catching her breath.

"Yeah, I was hoping to catch the bus, but..." She glanced at her watch, grimacing. "I suppose I've likely missed it now," she sighed, dejected. "I'll catch the next one, though. They run every half hour, so I've got time!" she laughed. Andre nodded, still smiling, then shrugged again.

"I could give you a ride, if you want," he said nonchalantly. Sarah stared at him a moment, then smiled hopefully.

"Really?" she asked. "I don't want to put you out, but if you could, I would really appreciate it..." Andre waved off her concern.

"Don't be ridiculous," he grinned. He held his arm out as he turned her back the way she'd come, ushering her in the direction of the parking lot. "I'm happy to do it. Besides," he winked, "it just means I get to spend a little extra time with you." Sarah laughed, adjusting the bag she had slung over her shoulder.

"Lucky you," she smiled ruefully. Andre reached over casually and took her bag from her, swinging it up onto his shoulder, instead. He stopped walking, and turned to look at her.

"Yes," he said, his hazel eyes growing serious. "Lucky me." Andre looked back over his shoulder, then gazed back into her eyes. Sarah caught her breath. *Uh oh,* she thought.

"Listen, Sarah," he began awkwardly, "I know it's none of my business, but...well...like, it's getting to be a nasty night out, and I know if you...that is, I never left you out in the cold to catch a *bus* home, if you know what I mean." Sarah groaned inwardly, but somehow managed to keep her annoyance from showing on her face.

"Andre," she explained patiently, "Sam *always* picks me up when we don't have class together, as I do her, but she had some errands to run today, and I told her not to worry about it. It was my choice, and it's no big deal. So relax!" Andre watched her carefully, seeming to consider something. He shrugged.

"If you say so," he replied, still serious. "I guess I just don't know what you see in that chick."

"It's not up to you, to see what I see," Sarah said quietly, not liking where this conversation was going at all.

"You can do better," Andre insisted. "You *deserve* better." He paused briefly, then spoke softly, pleading. "Please," he whispered, "give me another chance. I'll show you the kind of man I can be for you." Sarah gaped at him in disbelief.

"Give you another...what? Andre," she shook her head, "*we* were, like, two years ago..."

"A year and a half," he cut in. Sarah held up a hand, silencing him.

"Whatever," she sighed, then took his face in her hands and met his gaze evenly. "Look, the point is, I adore you, you know that, but I am in love with *Samantha*. I need you to at least try to start accepting that." Andre lowered his eyes, downcast.

"But you and I were so good together," he said sadly. Sarah smiled, brushing his hair from his eyes.

"We had fun," she agreed, "but..." Sarah cut off as Andre suddenly leaned in to kiss her. She pulled back and moved her hands to his shoulders, holding him off. "Andre, no," she said firmly, glaring at him. "Why would you...what's the matter with you? Why do you always start pulling that kind of crap with me? And why now?" Andre took an angry step back and glowered at her.

"Oh come on," he cried fiercely. "You know you're only with her 'cause she's a *stray*! You'll soon grow tired of her and come crawling back to me again, mark my words. She's become your little pet project, now, just 'cause her parents are dead!" Sarah's mouth fell open, and she shut it again, losing her patience.

"Okay, first of all...WOW. Thanks for that. Second, I'm with her because *I love her*, you arrogant idiot," Sarah yelled. "That's something you were never able to understand. People aren't possessions that you can just pick up and drop any time you feel like it, like you did with me." Andre tried to retort, but Sarah went on, ignoring him. "Sam respects me, and makes me feel loved and wanted every single day. Yes, you and I had fun together...a *long time ago*...but things have changed. *I've* changed. I want different things now. I want more. I *deserve* more. And Sam *is* more. She's everything." Sarah cut off, gasping, dimly aware that she had begun crying, but was too tired and upset to bother caring. She turned and began striding angrily back in the direction of the bus stop. Andre rushed to stop her as she reached the corner where she'd first literally run into him.

"Don't," he warned. "Think about what you're doing, because you won't get this chance again. When you're ready for someone who can be a real partner to you - your equal - I might not be there anymore. Just think about that for a second." Sarah glared at him.

"I don't need to think about it," she growled, grabbing her bag roughly from where it was still perched on his shoulder. "Now get out of my way. I'm going home. *And Samantha Collins is home to me.*" Andre glowered at her, but then shrugged as he stepped aside, letting her pass.

"Whatever, bitch," he muttered. "Your loss."

Sarah, her head down as she fought to control her tears, stormed around the corner - - - and saw her there, sitting frozen on the steps by the fire exit door, tears streaming silently down her face, and a bouquet of wild flowers - Sarah's favourite - held loosely in one hand. The wind whipped her hair wildly about her face, but Sam didn't move; didn't speak. She just sat there, taking Sarah in with a wide, blue-eyed stare.

In a flash of sudden realization, Sarah understood. Sam had come for her, after all, intending to surprise her after class. From the confused expression of mixed emotions on her face, Sarah guessed that Sam had heard every word of the exchange she'd had with Andre just around the corner.

Which meant that he had known that Sam had been there the entire time.

"Sam," Sarah whispered, watching as her girlfriend pushed

herself shakily to her feet. "I'm so sorry, honey." Sam's face crumpled, and Sarah's heart hammered in her chest. She dropped her bag to the ground as heavy raindrops began to fall, and wrapped both arms around Sam; crying with her as they both shivered in the cold.

"I love you, Sare," Sam whispered into her ear. "I love you so much. And you," she stammered, suppressing a sob, "you are home to me, too. Know that." Sarah nodded, unable to speak. She hugged Sam again, then kissed her deeply, feeling her own knees weaken despite the chill of the evening.

"I know, baby," she whispered. "I love you, too." She smiled then, brushing Sam's tears from her face. She tipped her head toward the flowers still clutched in Sam's hand. "Those for me, by chance?" she asked. Samantha nodded, and gave her a weak grin.

"By chance." Sarah's smile broadened as she accepted the bouquet.

"They're beautiful, lady," she said appreciatively. "As are you." Sam ducked her head, blushing slightly. "Now help me get these home. It's freezing out here!" Sam laughed then, and stooped to retrieve Sarah's bag from the swiftly dampening ground. She brushed it off, slung it over her shoulder, and took Sarah's hand. Together, they ran giggling through the cold rain of the darkening night, their brief drama with Andre now all but forgotten.

*   *   *

Emily didn't think she'd ever been so nervous. It was ridiculous. Her stomach was in knots, and her hands shook visibly while she tried to apply a hint of eyeliner; a trace of lipstick; to her already irrationally overheated face. Her cheeks were flushed; her usually straight short hair now softened by some slight curls. Her blue eyes sparkled at her reflection in the mirror. Nervous or not, even she had to admit that she didn't look half bad.

Her room was positively post-nuclear; the result of her earlier, panicked search through drawers and closets in a mad frenzy to find something to wear. Julie had come laughing to her rescue, dragging a simple yet elegant black dress into the fray and insisting that Emily try it on. *Every woman needs one*, she had said with a gleam in her eye. Jules had then explained that the dress had been one of Mom's, and that she'd never had the heart to shorten it to fit her better, so it had just hung unused in the spare room closet all these years. Forgotten completely, until now.

Emily had found that it fit her perfectly, and she ran a hand nervously, yet lovingly, along the smooth hem of its skirt. Closing her eyes, she pictured her mother wearing that same dress, how beautiful she must have felt, and how her father's eyes would have lit up the moment he saw her in it. Nearly unbidden, Ryan's face floated into her mind, his soft brown eyes twinkling as he smiled at her. *Good grief,* Emily thought, opening her eyes. *I feel sick.*

She turned back to the mirror, wondering how she would ever manage to get through dinner. She fixed her reflection with a determined glare.

"You're being ridiculous," she said to herself. "You've been out with him before, and it was fine. This isn't really any different." But it *was* different this time, she knew. For one thing, this time he had asked her, and he hadn't needed to. They'd gone for dinner before, of course, or long lunches when court had been in recess. Initially, they had always talked about the case but, over the years, their conversations had drifted into some of the more personal aspects of their lives. In some ways, Emily felt she already knew a good deal about Officer Ryan Mullen. But in other ways, she felt very much like a smitten teenager going out on her first date. At that thought, Emily caught her reflection blushing again, and rolled her eyes in disgust.

"Ridiculous," she muttered, snapping off the light and returning to her bedroom to grab her purse before heading downstairs. Emily had no sooner kicked some discarded clothing out of the way so that she could close the door on the chaos, when she heard the doorbell ring, causing her stomach to lurch anxiously. Trick began to bark excitedly.

"I'll get it!" Julie bellowed from the kitchen. Emily's eyes went wide and she made a move to rush down the stairs and intercept her sister, but realized that her purse had gotten snagged on her bedroom door handle, nearly causing her to lose her balance as it jerked her backward.

"Fine," she grumbled, tugging her purse free with a frustrated yank. "You get it." Emily heard the front door open, and Julie's animated chatter as she invited Ryan inside. Her sister's energy level had been up and down all week long, and Emily now suspected that Julie had been secretly saving some in reserve for just this sort of thing. She loved Jules to pieces, but it was times like this, when her sister would revel playfully in her discomfort - the air rife with possibilities involving her humiliation - that Emily would gladly strangle her. It seemed that no matter how many years had passed, how much older or more mature they became, there were times that Jules would succumb, gleefully, to her inner imp, and Emily braced herself for just such an encounter as she slowly descended the staircase.

She needn't have worried.

Ryan stood just inside the front door, politely making conversation with Julie, but he stopped dead the moment he laid eyes on her, his mouth falling open as he stared openly at her, then snapping shut again.

"You look amazing," he breathed. Emily smiled at him, enjoying his sudden nervous floundering, almost as much as she enjoyed how incredible he looked in his dark suit and long black overcoat. Julie grinned at her, and stepped to one side.

"Thank you," Emily said slowly, hoping she didn't sound as nervous as she felt. "You don't look so bad yourself!" she added, grimacing inwardly as the words left her mouth. This was going to be a long night.

"So, Ryan," Julie stepped in breezily, "where are you two kids headed tonight?" Ryan stood smiling at Emily a moment longer, then turned to Julie. He straightened, taking on a more formal tone.

"Well, Julie," he said in a deep voice, "I was thinking we would check out the new restaurant that just opened up down by the waterfront..."

"The Italian place?" Julie's eyebrows went up in an expression of impressed surprise.

"That's the one," he continued. "Then I thought maybe we'd go do a little dancing..." He glanced at Emily. "If that's okay with you?" Emily smiled again and nodded.

"That sounds lovely, Ryan," she replied.

"Hmm," Julie cut in, thinking aloud. "I didn't know cops could dance."

"Hey," Ryan said, pretended to be offended. "I've been known to cut quite a rug in my day, I'll have you know!' He tapped out a quick two-step in demonstration, as both women clapped, laughing. Julie rolled her eyes.

"Okay, I'll give you that, but 'cut a rug', really?! Tell me, Ryan, what was it like for you all, way back when the wheel was invented?" Julie asked, feigning wide-eyed interest. Emily grabbed her wrap from the closet and turned, laughing, toward the door.

"That's enough, Jules," she warned, a twinkle in her eye.

"Oh, well, the wheel!" Ryan joined in the banter effortlessly. "Good times, that was. Made working with a wheelbarrow that much easier, you know? Before, it had just been a barrow." His serious face broke into a boyish grin as both women laughed again. Julie put on her best little old lady voice, and mimed using a walker.

"Okay, well, then dearies," she said, ushering them to the door, "you'd best be off, then, I suppose. You have her home by 10pm sharp, young man, do you hear me?"

"Jules..."

"Oh yes, ma'am, absolutely, ma'am." Ryan said quickly, taking Emily's arm.

"Okay, 11pm, but not a minute later!" Julie heaved a heavy sigh. "I'll just be here, all alone, sleeping in my chair, waiting for you to bring home my sweet, beloved...oh, what did you say your name was again, dearie? I seem to have misplaced it..."

"I know where you sleep..." Emily laughed, tugging the door open, and gesturing at Ryan to go through first. He acquiesced immediately, and mimed a tip of his hat.

"Yes, ma'am," he said before he could stop himself. Emily frowned playfully.

"I can hurt you," she reminded him, and Ryan threw his head back in laughter. Emily winked at Julie, mouthed a silent '*thank you*' to her, and pulled the door closed behind her. They were on their way.

*   *   *

Julie rummaged around in the fridge, pulling out the various items she needed, and reorganizing the rest to make it all fit better. Thanksgiving had been over a week ago, and still they had far too much food crammed in there for just two people. They'd even sent some back with Sam and Sarah. Julie shook her head, smiling. Emily complained when she had to do it, but Julie felt she secretly enjoyed massive grocery shopping trips. Either that, or she was expecting she would have to one day fully equip a bomb shelter for them all, and she was getting in some practice ahead of time.

Cradling everything in her arms, Julie kicked the fridge door closed and carried her selected items to the counter island in the middle of the kitchen. She laid everything carefully out in front of her, taking stock as she did so. Laying two thick slices of fresh bread onto her plate, she reached for the butter, and scraped some off, spreading enough on each slice to create a thin but comprehensive layer; a barrier between the bread and the additional ingredients to come.

Next, she gently rapped the mayonnaise jar on the counter a few times to loosen it, then unscrewed the top and placed the lid on the counter next to her plate. Using her knife, she spread a much healthier layer on top of the butter, and wiped the knife clean-ish on the edge of the bread's crust. Now came the fun part.

Julie broke a few crisp leaves of lettuce off from the head, laying them flat onto one of the bread slices. On top of that, she added some sliced turkey (because she hadn't had enough of *that* over the holiday, apparently), which she'd picked up at the deli counter while shopping the

132

day before, and sprinkled a little salt and pepper on top, for added flavour. She picked up a block of cheese, and carefully cut off a few slices to add to her masterpiece. Finally, smiling in anticipation, Julie crossed over to the microwave and pulled out the bacon she'd stuck in there to reheat a few minutes ago. She layered the greasy goodness on top, and placed the second slice of bread in its rightful position atop the entire pile. A cold dill pickle on the side completed her creation, and she poured herself a glass of ginger ale with which to wash it all down. Trick had watched the entire process with growing interest from his spot in the corner, until he couldn't stand it anymore, and became her near-silent shadow as she moved about the kitchen, hoping that a scrap or two might fall happily his way if he just stayed close enough.

Quickly returning the remaining ingredients to the fridge, Julie gave the counter a quick wipe down before she sat at the table to eat her lunch. She knew Emily could be home at any time, and didn't want her walking into a mess, just in case Ryan was with her. The pair had seen each other more in the past week than they had in all of the last 25 years combined, it seemed, and their growing attraction to one another didn't show any signs of slowing down just yet.

Thinking about her sister, Julie grinned openly around a mouthful of heaven. *Damn, but I make a good sandwich*, she praised herself, momentarily distracted from her thoughts. Returning to the night Em and Ryan had gone out on what was technically their first date, Julie remembered how hard she'd laughed when her sister had returned to the house, hours later, as flushed and giddy as a schoolgirl. The two women had sat up late into the night, while Emily had spoken excitedly - and in nearly uncomfortable detail - about her evening. They'd gone to dinner, as planned, and Emily's initial nervousness had disappeared into a couple of glasses of wine. Ryan, being the driver, had of course abstained, but he had seemed determined to cater to Emily's every wish that night, and Emily, for her part, had been determined to let him.

They actually had gone dancing after, as well...or, at least, they had tried. The original hall that he had taken them to was all but deserted. They'd stayed long enough to realize that it wasn't going to get any livelier that night, and then Ryan had had an idea. Asking Emily to trust him, he'd driven them both to a roadhouse just outside of the city, right off the highway. Emily had never been there before, and had nervously wondered what she had gotten herself into, but Ryan had led her confidently by the hand as they'd rushed inside out of the cold.

The bar had been packed, with a live band performing well-known and popular cover tunes on a small wooden stage in the corner. People of all shapes and sizes were up on the crowded dance floor, singing along with the band and breaking into enthusiastic applause at the end of each song. Ryan had grinned at her and pulled her along behind him, heading straight to the dance floor. Emily had worried that they stood out too much, being that they were clearly over-dressed for the locale, but she quickly found that it had only served to win their acceptance, and they soon found themselves adopted into the fold as though they'd been regulars.

They'd spent hours dancing, laughing and shouting brief observations to one another over the music, as well as joining in when the audience members were asked to sing along with the band. Ryan had looked 10 years younger by the time they left, his hair drenched with sweat, cheeks rosy, tie hanging loosely around his neck, and shirt sleeves rolled up as high as they would go. His dark eyes had sparkled in the dim light of the roadhouse every time he had looked at her. And from the moment she'd descended the stairs wearing that dress, he'd had a very hard time taking his eyes off of her.

He'd driven her home, the two of them chatting and laughing the whole way, both voices already hoarse from the evening's entertainment. Ryan had then walked her to the door, and when she'd turned to thank him, he had suddenly bent over and kissed her. It was soft and hesitant at first, but had grown stronger as she'd kissed him back, her fingers running through the silky curls at the nape of his neck. Emily had invited him to come in that night, but Ryan had been a complete, if somewhat frustrating, gentleman, and had taken his leave, after seeing her safely inside.

Emily had run screaming upstairs to where Julie had been laying in bed, reading, and had breathlessly recounted it all for her like a sports commentator describing a particularly incredible play. Since then, Ryan had come by nearly every day to see her, and once they had even stayed in and all three of them had watched a double feature of DVD's together. Ryan had continued to be a gentleman, and had seemed genuinely touched when Emily, with Julie's blessing, had asked him to be a part of their Halloween tradition. He had respectfully declined, however, saying that he would drive them all to the cemetery, if they wanted, but that he would remain in the car, so that the girls could have their proper space and time with their parents. He had said that it wasn't his place to be more involved than that, and had added the word, 'yet', with a playful wink, before kissing Emily lightly and heading home.

With Halloween on her mind, and her lunch now finished, Julie stood and crossed the room to rinse her dishes in the sink. Sam and Sarah would be coming home tomorrow morning, hopefully early enough that they could all get their pumpkins carved and be at the cemetery before it got dark. There was still so much to do. Just then, Trick got up and trotted to the door, tail wagging, as Julie's ears picked up the sound of a car door closing. Emily was home. The two of them had a busy afternoon ahead of them, getting the house decorated for tomorrow, and she didn't want to waste any time. Julie dried her hands on a dishtowel, and made her way over to the door to greet her sister.

*   *   *

Sam raised her head, and looked around, taking a momentary but much needed break from carving. She smiled as she watched Sarah pursing her lips in thought, and Jules frowning down at her now-gutted pumpkin, a pencil tucked behind her ear. Emily, goggles from the previous pumpkin-gutting fiasco in the garage perched atop her head, stood in the doorway, rubber-gloved hands on hips, assessing whether or not they'd put down enough newspaper to protect against a large clean-up later. Every year, she worried about it. And every year, there was always more than enough. Sam wondered how her sister had managed to grow up to be such a clean freak, in the same house where Sam, now in her early 30's, still had to be reminded to remove her shoes when she came in from outside.

All of the women were hard at work carving their Jack-o'-Lanterns, and they each worked in relative silence, the only sound being the music playing softly in the background and the occasional sound of tools being used. From the corner of her eye, Sam noticed Sarah look her way, and turned to smile at her. Sarah smiled back, then got up and walked over to where Sam was working on her design. She'd designed

135

the template herself, and was really quite proud of it. Sarah stood over her a moment, her eyes moving from the template to Sam's partially-carved pumpkin, and back again.

"Can I ask you something?" Sarah said, finally. At Sam's nod, she continued. "Mine is nowhere near as complicated as this, but...I don't know...I keep getting turned around. How do you know which parts of your design to cut? How do you keep track of the parts that are supposed to stay dark? I keep wanting to cut those ones out, and leave the rest in. It's messing me up." Sam put down her knife and beckoned Sarah to sit down by her, eager to show her what she'd learned.

"Basically," she began, "you don't. You don't worry about the dark parts. Our dad always taught us...the trick is to carve the light." She grinned at Sarah's confused look. "See here," Sam continued, pointing to her template, "these parts here, the dark parts? They're pumpkin shell, essentially. They stay where they are. You don't touch 'em. What you want to do is take these other parts, the white ones, out. They're what the candle shines through to make the picture that people see, on the outside. So just keep telling yourself, don't touch the dark parts. Leave them alone. All you need to do is carve the light." She gazed at Sarah, watching to see if she understood what Sam was trying to say. At last Sarah looked back at her, nodding.

"Carve the light," she said, a slow smile spreading across her face. Samantha nodded with a grin of her own.

"Carve the light," she agreed. "My dad taught me that, so you can't go wrong."

Emily and Julie exchanged a knowing glance, smiled, and went back to work on their creations, while Sarah returned to her seat. She was now on a mission.

"Carve the light," she whispered, peering intently at her pumpkin. "Okay." She picked up her knife, and tentatively began cutting. Sam watched her a moment longer and then, smiling, went back to work.

*   *   *

Samantha gazed around the room, surveying everyone's

136

handiwork, a contented smile on her face. Even though they did this every year, as they had done for longer than Sam had even been alive, she never ceased to be amazed, amused, touched or flat out surprised by the Jack-o'-Lanterns that her sisters and she turned out each and every time. Every year it was different, and every year it somehow seemed better than the last. Each offering to the gods of Halloween - and to their parents - became more and more intent; more and more worthy; and they continued to pick up steam, rather than fade out and disappear.

This year was poised to do the same, and with the addition of Sarah's creation, all three sisters had agreed that their parents' love of the holiday would be sated once again, and that, even though they had all worked individually, their combined effort seemed to tally up to something more cohesive than any of them had ever imagined it would be.

Emily's contribution, to be left at their parents' graveside, was simple, yet elegant and deeply meaningful. She had carefully carved the unmistakable outline of a lit candle into the face of her Jack-o'-Lantern, which was intended to then be shadowed by the actual lit candle which would be placed inside. The idea, she explained, was to give their parents something to see by; a light to guide their way home. She managed to literally and figuratively carve the light this year, and Sam was very proud of Emily for coming up with the idea, and actually going through with it. Sam sometimes felt that Emily didn't realize her own worth; that she felt herself to be somehow lacking, and that she hid her true self - her true potential - away from anyone who could see it, in order to protect herself from feeling like a failure, and from getting hurt. By carving a candle into her pumpkin, Sam felt, Emily was finally taking on her destined role as a leader in the family. She was not only lighting their parents' way home but, Sam thought, Emily herself, in fact, *was* the light - for all of them. She was only just now beginning to realize it.

Julie's creation was similarly simple in its nature, and equally beautiful to behold. She had carved a long, forking tree branch into her pumpkin, winding its way from the back, around one side, across the front, and nearly meeting itself at the back, but finishing in a pointed end, instead. Upon one of the forks that branched near the front, she had carved a single solitary leaf, dangling precariously from its stem. It was a monument; a testament to the untenable veracity, and yet ultimate fallibility, of summer's last leaf. Julie's leaf would hold its post a little bit longer than the rest, but eventually it, too, would fall. Something about the solitude of that single leaf had always tugged at Sam's heart, and seeing the one carved by her sister's gentle hand made her feel all the more so the turning of the seasons; nature's indifference to the trials and tribulations of human existence. William Blake may have seen the world in a grain of sand, but to Sam, the world held its breath in that single, heart-stopping moment, in which one final fragile leaf lost its tenuous hold on the branch that had given it nourishment and life, from the instant of its creation, and fluttered to the ground, alone. Just looking at it was enough to bring Sam to tears.

Her own mild masterpiece was one she'd thought of before, but one she had been unable to work out the details of, until now. Guarding the house that year, and keeping watch over them all, her parents included, was Trick. Or, rather, a pumpkin-ized Trick-o'-Lantern, the template of which had taken her the better part of a day to create. She had worked tirelessly on the painstaking, tiny details, that would render Trick's face easily recognizable to anyone who stopped to have a look. Sam had wanted to work him into the tradition more, being that he was such a large part of their family, and she felt she had finally landed upon the perfect way to do so. She had made Trick his own pumpkin. Sam knew that, once he was lit up, the Trick-faced lantern would easily and safely light the way for them all.

Samantha turned her attention, finally, to Sarah's Jack-o'-Lantern, which made her heart swell with pride more and more even as she gazed upon it. Her idea had been simple, and yet it had been carried off with such quiet grace and beauty that Sam had trouble turning her eyes away from it. Sarah's contribution would also remain at the house, but Sam had the feeling that it should, perhaps, be shared with the world, in some way. She smiled to herself, wondering if she could possibly be more melodramatic. She just simply didn't feel that anyone could have captured the tone of the family that year better than Sarah had been able to manage. Her idea had been simple, and her message clear. Sam realized with a certain amount of pride that her girlfriend had also taken her advice on carving the light. Being listened to was something that Samantha wasn't always sure she would ever get used to.

Sarah had carved, simply, five rounded human bodies - like

138

gingerbread outlines, or paper dolls - and they each were joined at the hand, all winding around the back and sides of the pumpkin, almost like a vine, but with people. In the middle, at the front, instead of another person, the outlines were reaching out and holding a large, multi-dimensional and multi-layered heart. She had carefully carved her pumpkin to expose the gentle sloping curves of the heart, but had then added in something more akin to a 3-D effect, making the heart look like it was beating right out of the front of the Jack-o'-Lantern, connecting and completing the full circle of the human figures. Sarah told her that the figures represented her parents, her sister and herself, and that no matter whether their grip on one another was still strong after all these years, the important thing was that they were held together, ultimately, by their innate and all-encompassing love for one another.

Sam looked across the room at her girlfriend, who was watching her closely for her reaction, and smiled. It hadn't been a test, or anything, but if it had, Sarah had just passed with flying colours. It turned out, however, that she wasn't quite done writing the test; that she in fact had a little bit more to share. Taking Sam aside, Sarah led her into the kitchen where they could be alone for a moment, her blue eyes twinkling mischievously the whole time.

"What?" Samantha asked with a chuckle as she was being dragged along, "What's going on? What are you up to?" Sarah stopped suddenly and spun to face her, grinning widely from ear to ear.

"Okay," she giggled. "Close your eyes, and hold out your hands." Sam rolled her eyes.

"Oh dear, when you start with *that*, things almost never go well!" That brought a frown of disapproval from Sarah, to which Sam responded by doing what she had been told.

"No peeking," Sarah whispered, and Sam felt something drop into her outstretched hands. "Okay," Sarah said, standing back, "open your eyes." Sam complied, and looked down at what she was now holding. "I made it for you." Sarah said quietly.

It was a small gourd, that looked like a miniature pumpkin. Sarah had engraved a tinier version of the swirling, 3-D heart from her regular-sized Jack-o'-Lantern, into one side of the little gourd, and Sam traced it lovingly with one finger, momentarily unable to speak. She rolled the wee Jack-o'-Lantern over in her hands and there, engraved into the other side, she found the small "XO" that she and Sarah had always used to communicate with privately with one another, and she felt tears well up in her eyes.

"I love it, Sare," she whispered. "And you. Thank you so much, honey." Sarah grinned again, kissed her softly, and pulled her into a gentle hug.

"I love you, too, sweetie," she responded quietly.

~11~

Ryan arrived right on time to pick them up, and all four women piled into his car, Jack-o'-Lanterns in tow. Emily made a point of re-introducing him to Samantha and Sarah, stating that things were different now that she wasn't hiding the fact that she and Ryan knew each other much better than she had let on before. Sam had rolled her eyes and laughed, but gamely shook his hand again, anyway.

The ride to the cemetery was relatively brief, but the atmosphere inside the car gradually became more somber and quiet the closer the got to their destination. Julie placed her head against the cool glass of the window and closed her eyes; Sarah and Sam held hands and watched as the suburban landscape crawled past them outside. They drove through the gate and, following Emily's directions, Ryan drove them toward the small hill at the back end of the cemetery, where their parents' single headstone marked their final resting place. Tires crunching on the gravel roadway, Ryan pulled the car under a nearby tree and parked, shutting the engine off and pocketing the keys.

Silently, the women and Ryan climbed out of the car, and walked as a group over to the gravesite. Thick clouds had rolled in overhead, giving the afternoon a particularly gloomy appearance, and their breath as they walked hung in the chill of the air. The sound of their footsteps was dampened and dulled by the soft grass around them, and even the birds seemed to have taken the afternoon off, perhaps out of respect for those lost. Not a sound could be heard across the entire grounds.

Ryan and Sarah both bent to place flowers at the base of the headstones, then walked back a few steps to give the sisters some privacy; some time alone with their parents, and a chance to share uninterrupted space with one another. Sarah watched as each woman took a turn speaking, no doubt telling stories of how the events of the past year unfolded. She thought perhaps they would speak of their fears; of their hopes for the year ahead; of how much they missed their parents; of the battles fought and of the trials overcome. She watched as the new Jack-o'-Lanterns were unveiled and presented, each woman explaining the one they had carved, while the others adding in points that they thought were of notable importance. Sam and Sarah had left theirs at the house, to be lit when darkness fell, but Sarah smiled as she watched Sam attempting to describe them, motioning dramatically with her hands as she did so.

Each woman then, beginning with Emily, took a few minutes to be alone with their parents; to say what they wanted to say without worrying about how anyone else would react. Julie and Sam joined Ryan and Sarah while Emily spoke, and then she returned to let Julie go. Sarah watched as Jules took up a seated position on the cold, hard ground, picking idly at the grass beneath her as she spoke. Jules sat huddled there for quite awhile, but no one rushed her. Everyone understood that she deserved to take up however much time she required to say the things that she needed to say. When she did return, letting Sam go to have her turn, Julie seemed somehow even more tired and pale than she had when they'd left the house. Sarah noticed that she was shivering, and casually put an arm around her to help keep her a little bit warmer. She smiled up at Sarah gratefully, but Sarah could still sense the pain she was in, behind her eyes. Something was wrong. Julie was doing a valiant job of keeping it hidden from the surface, but whatever was bothering her seemed to be getting progressively worse. And it was happening more quickly. Even in the two weeks it had been since she'd seen her last, Sarah felt that Julie was somehow even smaller, paler and more frail-looking than she had been the weekend they'd first met. Julie was not okay, and everyone was avoiding it - most of all, Julie. She'd casually dismissed any concern or question regarding her health. Except Sarah's; that one and only time when Julie had admitted, privately, that she was not alright. Sarah frowned inwardly, deeply concerned, but opted to keep her thoughts to herself for the time being. There would be a time and a place to further discuss whatever was going on, but this was not it.

When Julie returned, it was obvious that she had been crying, and Sarah wondered at how much truth Jules had just revealed to her parents, that was still basically unknown to her two sisters.

"I have to talk to you about something," Julie announced in a quiet voice. "Later, after the candy is all handed out, okay?" Both women nodded, mutual expressions of confusion and fear on their faces, but neither challenged the timeline that had just been set. Julie would tell them what she wanted to tell them when she was ready, and not a moment sooner. Sarah caught her eye and Julie met her questioning gaze with a slight nod, which no one else seemed to notice. Emily simply hugged her, and Samantha started off to have her turn alone with her parents. She'd taken only a few steps, then turned back to them, a curious look on her face.

"Would it be okay if...can I introduce them to Sarah?" Emily and Julie looked at one another, then over at Sarah. Emily shrugged.

"I don't see any reason why not," she replied. "I think it's a pretty great idea, actually!" Sam held out her hand, and Sarah moved hesitantly forward to join her.

"I'm not sure if..." she began, but Sam cut her off.

"Please," she pleaded quietly. "It's important to me." Seeing the look in Sam's blue eyes, Sarah nodded her agreement, and the pair headed over together, hand in hand. They stopped in front of the headstone, and Samantha plopped easily onto the ground, pulling Sarah down with her. They sat together in silence for a moment, Sam resting her chin on her knees. She seemed to be thinking carefully, trying to find a way to word what she wanted to say. Despite the cold, Sarah waited patiently, knowing that Sam often needed to take her time finding the words she needed to express herself. It was part of what made her such an amazing writer. Samantha sighed heavily, and started in slowly, as if feeling her way in the dark.

"Mom, Dad," she began hesitantly, "this is Sarah, the woman I was telling you about. I brought her here today so she could meet you, and so you could see the kind of person that she is. Just wait until tonight, when you see the pumpkin she carved for you...for all of us. She just gets it...gets me...gets *us*. I think you'd be proud...I think you'd like knowing her, almost as much as I do. I hope you would be, anyway. I hope you wouldn't be...I mean...I know she's probably not who you would have maybe pictured for me, but she's smart, and she's beautiful, and she makes me laugh...so much. Even on those days when I don't think there's any laughter left in me. She calms me, and reminds me to breathe. She takes care of me. And she loves me. And I love her. She makes me happy, inside, in ways I never really thought I ever would be. I'm not sure if you knew that...if you could ever tell...I was sad a lot, lonely a lot, even before you were taken from us. It was always there, you know? It sat inside me like a black hole, sucking happy moments away almost before I knew they were there, sometimes. And Sarah...she's like the balance to that, you see? If you can see inside of me, right now, you'd see that the hole gets filled up with smiles. She makes me feel safe. And I'm not so lonely anymore. I don't know how to..." Sam swallowed with a sob. "I need to know that it's okay...that you wouldn't be...angry. Or disappointed. Or...I don't know...I just need it to be okay. Because, aside from you guys and my big sisters, Sarah is about the most important person on the planet to me. She has my heart, and she's taking excellent care of it. I guess I just...I was hoping...that we could maybe have your blessing? I hope we would. Em and Jules say it's without a doubt, but I guess I just...hope. I hope we do. Because I'm happy, truly happy, for the first time in my life. And I have to believe that you would be okay with that. I need to believe that, okay?"

Samantha sniffled at wiped at her nose, still thinking. Sarah reached over and put a reassuring arm around Sam's shoulders, furtively brushing a tear from her eye, as well. She hadn't been expecting any of that, and realized that she suddenly felt much closer to her girlfriend than she had before. It was as if she could see her better now, more clearly. And it made her love her all the more. Sam coughed briefly, then continued in a quiet voice, following the swirling train of her thoughts.

"I don't remember a lot, you know," she explained. "About them, I mean. Like, Em and Jules have been amazing at telling me the same stories over and over...I pretty much know them all off by heart. But...knowing the story isn't the same as remembering the event, you know? I sometimes feel like my memories are gone, and were replaced with theirs, because theirs are so much better...richer...more detailed. I can picture things, sometimes, but it's not the same as having the memory be your own. I do remember some stuff, though. What I remember most about my mom are her hands. I loved her hands. I used to watch her do things...I used to sit and watch her cooking...baking. I remember her rolling out cookie dough, for example. She used to make these pinwheel

144

cookies at Christmas time. I tried to help, once, but I was too small to do it very good. And I wasn't any help putting icing on her shortbread cookies...I ate more than what made it onto the cookie top. But one year, when I was finally big enough, she let me help her make these thumbprint cookies...you put your thumbprint in a little dough ball, and fill it with jam after. They were so good! My thumbs were still pretty small, so she had to help, but I was good at rolling the dough," Sam nodded. "That was one of my favourite things...just being alone with her, and watching her hands while she worked. I think I remember her hands better than I do her face, sometimes." Sam closed her eyes.

"My dad is harder to remember," she said quietly. I don't think we did anything like that, just the two of us, you know? I mean, looking back, he was one man in a house full of women. There was no one tossing the football with him out in the yard, or helping fix the car, or grilling on the BBQ. He was the only man, and he did all that stuff pretty much on his own, alone. And yet he was so patient with us...his girls. Em said he taught her to change a tire before she got her license. And he was always available to help Jules with homework and science projects. But I was so young..." she cut off, unable to speak momentarily. "We just didn't get to do much that was just us, you know? I do remember some things, though," she confessed. "I remember his laugh. He had a great laugh...a real genuine laugh. The kind that, when you hear it, it makes you want to laugh, too. He always seemed so big to me, but when I made him laugh, it's like we were the same size for a moment. Like we were almost the same person, in that we'd shared the same humorous moment together. God, I remember how I loved to make him laugh," Sam smiled.

"He used to carry me upside-down to bed, by my feet!" Sam giggled, and in that moment, Sarah caught a brief glimpse, as she so often did, of the little 7-year-old girl that Sam had once been, reduced to helpless giggles at being swung upside-down by her seemingly monolithic father as he went to tuck her into bed at night. Sarah saw that child in her quite clearly, however fleeting though it may be, and it made her heart ache, as she smiled simultaneously. Sam had grown quiet, then, and Sarah glanced at her to make sure she was okay. Sam was gazing back at her, an unreadable expression on her face.

"Thank you for coming here," she whispered.

"Thank you for having me," Sarah whispered back. "Are you okay, sweetie?" Sam blinked more tears back, then nodded.

"Yeah," she said. "I think I am maybe more okay than I've been in a long time." She glanced back at the car, to where her sisters and Ryan were waiting for them. "We should get going," she said, standing up, and offering a hand to Sarah. "I'm getting worried about Jules. She doesn't look so good."

Sarah let Sam pull her to her feet, then turned to look at the others, as well, brushing bits of grass from her jeans. Samantha was right; Julie didn't look very good at all. She was leaning against the car, looking either very tired, or very much in pain, or both. Unbelievably, she'd turned even paler as the afternoon wore on. She turned back to Sam and nodded.

"Let's go," she agreed. "We'll help get the Jack-o'-Lanterns lit, and then get Jules home to rest for a bit. Okay?" Sam nodded, and the two women turned together and headed back in the direction of the car. Neither spoke on the short walk back, both wrapped up in their own concerned thoughts, as they were. It was turning out to be a very long and emotionally overwhelming afternoon.

*   *   *

Back at the house, Julie went to lie down and rest some more, while Emily set about preparing an early dinner. Ryan had decided to stay, and was helping Samantha and Sarah finish the remaining decorations out in the yard. Trick had been happy to see them return, of course, so he was outside, too, running off some of his energy. Emily was so absorbed in her own thoughts and questions about their annual trip to the cemetery, so different from any other, that it almost didn't register when she first heard it, despite how quiet the rest of the house had been.

A dull, muffled *thump* had come from upstairs. It sounded almost like it had come from the direction of Julie's room. Emily paused, straining to listen. No further sounds came to her, however, and she started back to work chopping up vegetables for the steamer. She paused again, thinking. *Had* she heard something? She hadn't really been paying attention, so she couldn't be sure. A cold knot began to tighten, deep down in her stomach. She put the knife down on the cutting board and rinsed her hands in the sink, drying them off on her jeans.

It's probably nothing, she thought. *But it can't hurt to go up and check, just to be sure.*

Emily climbed the stairs quietly, not wanting to disturb Julie if she had managed to fall asleep. Though, what she would say if she got caught skulking up the stairs right then, Emily wasn't sure. She was just going to take a quick peek around, and go back down to the kitchen. She just wanted to be sure.

She got to the top of the stairs and paused again, listening. Nothing. Emily was feeling silly, but decided that, since she had gone that far, she may as well go all the way. She rounded the corner into the hallway...and stopped dead. Julie's door was open a crack, the dwindling sunlight still managing to cast shadows from her room out into the hall. Emily peered at the open doorway, a frown crinkling her brown. Something didn't look right. The cold knot inside of here tightened some more.

She continued as quietly as possible down the hall, and reached for Julie's doorknob, intending to pull it shut. But the moment she put her hand on the knob, she knew without a doubt that something was wrong. The handle was cold to the touch, and Emily could detect a slight breeze coming from inside the room. She eased the door open quietly and gasped, her mind barely registering the wide open window as it instead processed the horror in front of her. Julie was lying face down on the floor, and she was not moving.

"Julie?" Emily called softly, and then again, much louder. "Jules?" Julie didn't respond. Emily rushed forward and knelt next to her sister, terrified tears streaming from her eyes. "Jules!" she shouted. "Wake up!" Emily shook her. Still no response from her sister.

"No," Emily cried, "Oh Jules, no no no no no...." Emily leapt to her feet and raced back to the hallway, screaming as loudly as she could. "SAM!" she shrieked. "SA-AM! Oh my God, Sam...call 9-1-1! Hurry!" Sobbing, Emily rushed back to her sister's side and fell to her knees beside her. She gently rolled Julie over, cradling her head in her arms.

"Please wake up, Jules," she whispered helplessly. "Please..."
Emily began to rock her tenderly, kissing the top of her head, and
praying. The others rushed in from outside, and after quickly assessing
the scene, Ryan calmly called for help. Sarah wrapped her arms tightly
around a near-hysterical Samantha, and together they waited as Emily,
holding her unconscious sister, rocked her and whispered over and over.

"Please hang on, Julie," she breathed. "Please..." Emily wept
quietly as the sound of the oncoming sirens drew ever closer. *We're
running out of time*, she thought. *Please don't let it be too late.*

*   *   *

Samantha stared at the doctor, unable to believe what she was
hearing. *It's not possible*, her mind screamed. *There must be some kind of
mistake.*

When the ambulance had arrived, Julie had briefly regained
consciousness, muttered something largely incoherent about candy, and
had passed back out again. Emily had ridden with her to the hospital,
while Ryan had followed closely behind with Sam and Sarah. Together,
they had waited what seemed an agonizingly long time for the doctor to
come out and let them know what was wrong. Emily was pale with
unspoken fear, absently wringing her hands and running her fingers
through her hair as she paced the waiting room. Ryan finally stepped in
and got her to sit down, bringing her a bottle of water from one of the
vending machines. Sam sat next to Sarah, afraid to speak. She just kept
looking from the door they'd taken Julie through on a gurney, over to
Emily, and back again. She was afraid to breathe, feeling that it would
somehow break something in the air if she were to breathe too deeply.
Sarah sat next to her, quietly, holding her hand. Every so often, she would
nervously bite her lip, but otherwise, Sarah was a calm centre in the midst
of Samantha's inner storm. Together, they waited like that for what
seemed like endless hours.

Finally, the doctor had come out, and asked them to follow her to
her office. She didn't appear to be much older than Emily, with a kind and
sincere face and golden hazel eyes. She led them to a nearby office area
and prompted Ryan and Sarah to wait outside, while she spoke with
Emily and Sam alone. That had made Samantha feel very nervous, but
she'd complied without argument, kissing Sarah on the cheek before

following Emily inside. Both women took seats opposite a large wooden desk, and glanced at one another nervously in a frightened daze.

The doctor had begun speaking, and Sam had not understood, at first, what she was talking about. She was saying something about Julie's "condition" and the "rapid spread of the disease" contributing to her losing consciousness for a time. Emily, her frustration increasing with each passing moment, abruptly cut the doctor off mid-sentence.

"Excuse me, " she interrupted, "I'm sorry, but I'm not sure what you are talking about." Emily took a deep breath. "What - condition?" she asked. "What's wrong with our sister?"

The doctor had paused then, peering at them carefully before answering.

"She didn't tell you," the woman said, realization dawning in her eyes. Emily and Sam had exchanged glances, and shaken their heads, anxiously waiting for her to continue. The doctor sighed, somewhat sadly, Sam thought. *She didn't tell us.* Sam ran over the doctor's words again in her head. *She said she wanted to talk to us. She just didn't get the chance.* Samantha felt her eyes well up with tears, and she reached over, suddenly needing to take Emily's hand. Her sister squeezed her hand desperately in return, refusing to let go. They both inhaled as one, and released their collective breath slowly. The doctor leveled them with a steady gaze. The next words out of her mouth would change their lives forever.

Cancer, she had said, her face so gravely serious that Sam felt her stomach drop immediately, as Emily's hand tightened on hers. Julie was no longer in remission. Her cancer had come back - with a vengeance - and she had kept it from them both, apparently for months. Sam felt crushed, and continued to grip Emily's hand as though it were her only lifeline, keeping her from tumbling over the edge into an endless abyss. At that moment, her older sister felt like the only stable thing in an otherwise swirling-off-kilter world to her.

Both women had argued with the doctor's bleak diagnosis for their sister, of course. Sam had been in angry tears of denial, screaming at the woman until her voice went hoarse. There must be something they could do. Emily had remained pale; quiet; in shock. Sam wondered briefly if Emily had felt that everyone was leaving her; deserting her. But Samantha's mind - every cell of her body - was railing against the grim scenario that this doctor was presenting to them as an inevitability.

Jules was dying. The disease was spreading rapidly, and there was nothing anyone could do to stop it.

"No," Sam cried, "there has to be something...we have to *do* something!" The doctor leveled a gaze at her.

"What you can do," she said slowly, "is to take her home, make her as comfortable as possible, and be there for her as only you can." An uneasy silence fell over the small room. Sam opened her mouth to object, tears streaming down her face, but Emily spoke first.

"Okay," she said quietly, nodding slowly to herself as she calmly wiped tears from her eyes. "Then that's what we'll do." Emily stood decisively, reaching out to pull Sam to her feet, as well. "Could we please see her now? We need to go be with our sister."

*   *   *

Julie forced her eyes open, squinting into the dim light. She was aware that other people were in the room - she'd heard their low voices whispering off and on as she'd drifted in and out of consciousness. She felt terrible, and was having trouble focusing, as though her mind - and the entire world, in fact - were filled with thick layers of cotton. She blinked, trying to discern some of the identifying details of her current surroundings. Julie had no idea where she was. She realized that she couldn't remember what had happened - they'd been at the cemetery, she'd gone upstairs to lie down once they'd arrived back at home, and then - nothing. Her mouth was dry, and she licked her lips, trying to generate some bit of moisture.

"She's awake," she heard Emily say quietly from somewhere nearby, and she sensed other people moving closer to her bedside. Julie forced her eyes open again (*When did I close them?*, she wondered absently), peering hazily at the shadows around her. Emily's face slowly drifted into focus, followed by Samantha's. Dimly, Julie could discern Sarah and Ryan standing further away, near the foot of the bed she was lying in. It wasn't her bed, though, that much she knew. She was in a hospital. Sam was in tears, and everyone else's faces were tight with worry and concern. Emily looked as though she may collapse into a panic at any given moment. Julie closed her eyes briefly, sighing heavily, and she felt all of the struggle of pretense fall away from her shoulders.

They knew.

"I'm sorry," she croaked. Emily wiped a tear off her cheek and took Julie's hand, as Samantha collapsed into whimpering sobs on the other side of the bed.

"No Jules," Emily whispered, shaking her head sadly. "You have nothing to be sorry about. I can't..." Emily swallowed hard, her eyes moving to look helplessly out the window for a moment, then returned to meet Julie's face. "I can't believe you've been carrying this all by yourself all this time." She reached down and tenderly brushed Julie's sweat-soaked hair back off her forehead. "But we're here now. You're not doing this alone anymore."

Julie nodded and closed her eyes again, feeling a tear escape her own eye and trickle slowly down her cheek as she did so. She was so tired, and felt sleep coming for her once again, as Sam sniffled loudly and took her other hand.

"Em's right, Jules," she whispered as Julie drifted off. "We're here now. And we're not going anywhere."

*   *   *

The following months were filled with the chaos of change and alteration. Emily eventually hired a part-time nurse to stay with Julie while Emily was at work, thus allowing Julie to remain at home as much as possible while her health swiftly declined. Samantha and Sarah made the trip back from school as often as time and finance would allow, but by the time their Christmas break rolled around, both girls had mutually decided to put the rest of their program on hold for the second term, and had moved in with Emily and Julie for the remainder of the school year.

The holidays passed by almost unnoticed, leaving the women in a somber mood as they entered the new year. Ryan became a regular fixture in the household, arriving nearly every day after his work shift was through, and often spending the night, as well. Emily found herself taking great comfort in his quiet strength, and found him to be invaluable when she became too caught up in caring for and worrying about Julie to remember the little necessities like groceries and bill payments. His calm presence around the house cemented her growing affection for him, as he openly and wordlessly became a member of their newly expanding family.

Days and weeks passed into months, and as they moved into mid-March, Julie came down with what started off as a simple cold, and ended up landing her in the hospital once again. Emily had heard her up coughing one night, and went to check on her. Finding her unable to draw anything close to a full breath, Emily had woken Sam and Sarah, and the three of them, in terror, had rushed Julie to the hospital, calling Ryan along the way to meet them there, which he did, arriving just a few shaky minutes after they did. The doctor was concerned with how hard the virus had hit and defeated Julie's weakening immune system, and had kept her bedridden in intensive care for nearly two weeks. The girls had been terrified, unsure as to whether they would ever be able to take Julie home again, but the doctor had finally relented, and released Julie into her sisters' care, on the condition that the nurse be moved to full-time, live-in status to help them keep her more comfortable as spring approached, and her condition worsened.

Emily and Samantha managed to have Julie home for her birthday, however, and the girls all went out of their way to make it as special and as memorable as possible for her. Together, and with Sarah's help, they had cobbled together a scrapbook photo album of their family through the years, from the time Emily and Julie had been small, all the way through to include recent photos from Halloween and the holiday season of the previous year. Sarah had patiently taught Emily how to scan and colour correct old pictures, slides and negatives, while Sam had created unique borders, notes and memory bubbles throughout the rapidly growing album. She and Emily included short letters to their sister, which reminisced on certain special memories that they'd each shared with her. Additionally, each of the girls, and Ryan, had traced the outlines of their hands, and glued them into the interior of the book, with a photo of each attached to the palm. Not to be left out, Trick also got his paw print traced and added to a page, and surrounded by photos from when he was a puppy, up to and including one random shot that Sam had taken of him while Julie was still in the hospital. When she'd opened her gift, Julie had poured carefully over each and every detail, smiling to herself while whimsical tears alternately traced their way down her cheek. She'd embraced her sisters tightly, telling them all that it was absolutely the greatest gift she'd ever received.

Emily had baked cupcakes instead of one big cake, hoping that Julie would at least be able to enjoy even a small part of her favourite chocolate-y goodness, if she was up to it, on her actual birthday. For her part, Julie was exhausted, but game, and grinned happily as everyone present sang happy birthday while a single candle burned atop her portion. She closed her eyes, made a wish, and blew the candle out, smiling at the resulting applause, before dipping her finger into the icing and licking it off gleefully. Emily rolled her eyes in mock disgust.

"God, we can't take you out *anywhere*," she scolded with a laugh. She winked at Ryan, who grinned back at her. "Kids these days," she sighed. Julie laughed, then licked her finger again, clearing her throat thoughtfully.

"I won't tell you my wish, or it won't come true," she said in a quiet voice, "but there is another wish I have, that can only be fulfilled by someone in this room."

"Well, it's your birthday," Sarah piped in, "I vote that you get as many wishes as you want!"

"Yeah, little sister," Emily agreed with a nod. "Name it." Julie looked weakly around the room, laying her head back in her pillows for a moment, before she raised it again and looked directly at Samantha.

"I wish..." she began, hesitating slightly, then continuing. "I wish I knew why you ran out that night." A hush fell over the room. All eyes turned on Sam, who had gone visibly pale, her eyes wide and staring back at Julie.

"What..." Sam began, taking a slow step backward. She looked suddenly stricken. "I- don't...I don't know..." Her voice trailed off as she took another step back. Her eyes flicked nervously toward the doorway, and she sagged, appearing disheartened, as Emily casually stepped in the way of her only escape route. Samantha shook her head, slowly at first,

153

and then more rapidly. "No," she moaned softly. "I don't...please...I don't know..."

"You do," Julie whispered quietly, not taking her eyes off of her younger sister. It felt as though time itself had paused to listen; as if the world were holding its breath, waiting to see what would happen. "You do know," Julie said gently. "You've just been running from whatever it is for the past 25 years, and you need to stop now, or it will eat you alive, sweetie. It will. Trust me on this one, okay? Just let it go...let it out, and let it go. And then it can't hurt you anymore. And we'll be right here...whatever it is, we'll be here to help you..."

"No," Sam interjected, panic in her eyes. "No, you won't...it's...you don't know..." She choked back a sob and pressed her back up against the wall, unable to go any further. "Please," she pleaded in a low voice. "Please...don't make me do this. Anything but this, Jules - please..." Julie shook her head sadly and Sam covered her face with her hands, weeping quietly to herself.

"Please just trust me, Samie," she replied. "Trust *us*. We're your sisters; your family. Please tell us what you're running from...let us help you." Sam continued sobbing quietly into the silence of the room. Julie waited a moment, watching her, then pressed her sister again. "We were trick-or-treating," she reminded Sam gently. "We came back, and the police were already here, talking to Emily." Sam continued to hold her hands over her face, refusing to meet anyone's eyes, but it was clear that she was listening. Julie pushed herself up a little more in her bed, peering intently at her sister. "But that's not when you ran," she went on, "and that's what I never understood. You were upset, as we all were, but we were all in the living room together...trying to somehow fathom what was happening. We were all together. And then all of a sudden, you just...took off. It seemed to come from nowhere, Samie. You just up and ran, and I could never figure out why..."

"Why?!" Sam screamed suddenly, slamming her fists on the wall behind her and turning her tear-stained glare on Julie. "You want to know? You want the reason?" Sam was panting; raging. Julie watched her calmly for a moment before responding.

154

"I do," she whispered. "I want to know the reason why you ran away. After all these years, I want to know. I want you to tell me what caused it." Sam glared at Julie, who waited patiently to see what her response would be. Emily, still blocking the door, watched as the drama unfolded in front of her, afraid to breathe. Ryan and Sarah had all but melted into the walls in an effort not to intrude. All eyes were locked on Samantha, waiting. Sam shook her head and pounded the wall once more, then clapped her hands harshly against the sides of her head, as if trying to beat a writhing snake back down into trapped submission within her own mind.

"The cause," she cried, staring at the floor. "The cause...I caused...my f - I - did it. It was me...before...before we went out..." Samantha doubled over as her body was racked with a fit of coughing. Julie frowned slightly, confused.

"Before we went out? Before...trick or treating...?" Sam nodded, crying, still refusing to look at anyone in the room. She almost appeared to be in her own world; her memories taking her back to that one horrible night. The night everything had fallen apart for the Collins family. The night Samantha first began to run.

"I don't understand," Julie said quietly, still confused. "What happened before we went out? There was nothing..."

"Everything!" Sam pounded the wall again, as though emphasizing her point. "Everything happened! I - I didn't want..." She broke down into another fit of choking sobs before continuing in a quiet voice. "I didn't want to go," she whispered. "I didn't want to be a princess or whatever it was. Remember? I wanted to be Spiderman. And I was so mad because Mom made me wear your old costume from some stupid play, instead. Some stupid dress. Spiderman didn't wear a dress. I wanted to be him, and she wouldn't let me. And I was mad."

Everyone in the room remained silent and still, listening. Samantha was so caught up in her own memory, still staring at the floor, that she didn't notice Emily take a small, careful step in her direction, while Ryan moved silently to cover the door in her place. They each hardly dared to breathe. Everyone simply watched, waiting for her to continue. Samantha's face crumpled in despair.

"It wasn't even so bad, you know? In the end? I actually kind of felt kind of pretty, in the end. But, before that, before we went out...I was so angry. At her, at you, at the costume, at all of it. I was so, so mad. And I was determined to show them...to show you all. I was little and no one was listening to me, so I wanted to make them listen. I wanted everyone to know that I was mad. I remember, I was yelling and running and I slipped. In the kitchen, remember? I slipped. And I...I..." Sam cut off a moment, choking back another round of sobs. Suddenly, Emily's quiet voice broke the silence.

"You dumped the cupcakes," she said in a slowly, remembering. "You slipped and grabbed the counter, only you pulled down the tray of cupcakes Mom had made to take to the party they were going to. The chocolate pumpkin ones. They fell and the container landed upside-down, on its lid. She had to re-ice almost all of them before they could leave..." Emily's gaze flicked suspiciously over to Samantha, who was staring back at her intently, as though willing her to see - to understand. Emily didn't.

"But...she wasn't angry, or anything," Emily said quietly, shaking her head in confusion. "They weren't angry with you, when they left. I remember that Mom even joked about how the cupcakes had been Sam-ified. It was cute. They were smiling. They weren't mad - just a bit late, and it didn't really matter..." Sam's sudden gasp of anguish cut her off.

"That was ALL that mattered!" she cried, sobbing harder. "I know they weren't mad. Mad wasn't the problem. The problem is that they were *late*. I made them late!" Sam spun on Ryan, pointing a finger at him, as her other hand strayed to her clutch absently at her abdomen. "That woman," she said hoarsely. "That woman you were with...what's her name...?" Sam shook her head, her tear-streaked face wincing at some sight unseen; some thought unheard. "Doesn't matter," she muttered, waving her hand in a dismissive gesture. "She said...she said it..." Sam cut off crying, and Emily took another step closer to her, looking perplexed.

"What, Samie," she asked gently, glancing briefly at Julie, who had gotten even paler. She looked just as confused as Emily felt, but she was listening so intently that Emily thought maybe Jules was on the verge of some sort of realization. She returned her attention to Samantha. "What did she say, sweetie?" Sam was breathing heavily, shaking her head sadly.

"She said...she..." Sam hesitated, then closed her eyes and let her head drop back to rest against the wall behind her. "She said they were in the wrong place...at the wrong time." She cut off, pressing a white-knuckled fist to her mouth and swallowing briefly before continuing. "The wrong time," she whispered sadly. Sam raised her eyes to look from Emily to Julie and back again. Seeing that they still didn't quite get it, Samantha tried again. "Don't you see?" she asked, pleading with them to understand. "They were in the wrong place at the *wrong time*. If they'd left on time...if I hadn't made them late...then they wouldn't have..."

"Oh my God," Julie whispered, comprehension dawning on her face. "No...Sam..."

"It's my fault!" Samantha cried. "I did it! I made them late and it's my fault they're dead now! I did it! I'm the reason!" Sam collapsed in tears as Emily reached her; catching her sister just in time to keep her from falling to the floor. She wrapped both arms around Sam, and held her as they slid to a seated position, her back against the wall, unable to believe what she'd just heard.

"Is *that* what you think?" she asked as Sam clutched at her, burying her face into Emily's shoulder. "Sweetie, no..." Emily felt tears cascading down her face. How could she have been so blind? All this time, Samantha had been carrying guilt that wasn't hers, and none of them had had any idea. She'd sensed that something was wrong, of course, but she'd never even suspected anything like this. Not like this. Emily held her sister tightly, as she had that horrible night, feeling Sam's grief and despair pour out of her with each wrenching sob. Dimly, she was aware that Julie and Sarah were also crying, and she wiped absently at her nose as she pulled Samantha's face back so that she could look her in the eye. Sam fought back, but Emily remained firm.

"Samie, no," she said steadily, holding her sister's face in her hands. "That's not the way it works, kiddo. What happened was an accident. No one could have seen it coming, and there was nothing any one of us could have done to stop it." Sam shook in her arms, her wide blue eyes staring into the grim memory she'd kept locked within her mind.

"The wrong time," Sam whispered. "I made them...it's my fault..."

Her face crumpled again, and suddenly Ryan was there, kneeling down next to them. He cupped his hand under Sam's chin and gently turned her head to face him.

"It was an accident, Sam," he explained patiently. "You did not cause it. It is not your fault. You are not to blame. That's not what Pam meant when she said they were in the place at the wrong time." Sam's sobs renewed at the memory of that moment, and Ryan placed his hands gently on either side of her face, locking her in his strong, steady gaze. "Did you mean it?" he asked her suddenly. Sam blinked, surprised at the question.

"Mean...it...what?"

"Did you mean to dump the cupcakes?" he pressed quietly. Sam shook her head slowly. "No," he whispered.

"You didn't. Did you want them to be late? Did you try to make them leave late?" Sam sniffled, shaking her head. "No," he agreed. "Did you want them to die?" Sam gaped at him.

"No," she said quietly, staring at him. "No, I never wanted..."

"No," he said, cutting her off. "No, you didn't intend to dump the cupcakes. No, you didn't want them to be late. And no, even though you were angry, you did not want them to die." He took a deep breath, letting it out slowly, and brushing another tear from Sam's face with his thumb as Emily held her, shivering, in her arms. "The truth is, Samantha, that what happened that night was truly an accident. There was nothing anyone could have done. The only person at all responsible was the man driving the other car. The arrogant rich kid looking for some thrills. He got in over his head, wasn't thinking clearly at all, and he made a series of very bad choices. Choices that he can't take back. Choices for which he has paid dearly over the past 25 years. But they were his choices, Sam. His mistakes. Not yours. What happened wasn't because of anything you did, you understand? What happened was a terrible tragic accident. But it was just that. An accident. And you are not to blame. At all. You are no more to blame for what happened than I am, for not getting to the scene sooner. Do you understand? It wasn't your fault."

Sam blinked at him, trying to reconcile what he was saying with what she had believed all of her life. Julie coughed then, and everyone turned to look at her. She was looking from Ryan to Sam to Emily, processing everything she'd just heard.

"Sam, honey," she croaked. "How could you...why didn't you ever say anything about this before?" Sam turned to look at her, her eyebrows furrowed in concentration.

"Because," she whispered reluctantly. "I didn't want you to hate me." Julie stared at her, then pushed herself up in bed, turning to slide her legs out, gingerly placing her bare feet on the floor. Carefully, she picked her way across the room, holding onto the side of the bed for support, and knelt in front of Samantha, brushing her hair back off her face as Sam glanced at her timidly.

"I....we...could *never* hate you, do you understand?" Julie held her gaze evenly. "You are our sister. And you're everything we never were. We love you, Samie. Always. I can't believe that you've been carrying something like this on your own for so long. I guess," she glanced at Emily, "I guess we all needed to learn to let things out once in a while, huh?" She stroked Samantha's hair softly. "No more secrets, kiddo, okay? Not for any of us. We're all we have, so no more. Secrets are banned, okay?" She looked at both women in turn as she spoke. Emily and Sam nodded slowly, sniffling.

Julie pulled both of her sisters into a tight hug, which they returned. Emily felt Ryan's hand on her shoulder, and put one arm around him, as well. Julie kissed Samantha's hair, and reached back toward where Sarah had been standing near the far wall, bearing witness to every moment. Sarah grabbed her hand and Julie pulled her into the circle as well, smiling to herself as Trick continued trying to wedge his way into the centre for his share of the affection. She kissed the top of Sam's head again, and exhaled shakily.

"Thank you for making my birthday wish come true," Julie whispered with a sigh. "I love you all, so so much."

*   *   *

~Epilogue~

Julie passed away later that summer, on a peaceful but rainy afternoon. She had been able to remain at home, as she'd wanted, and Samantha had been at her side, alone. Sensing that the moment they'd been fearing was drawing near, Sarah had stepped out quietly to get Emily and the nurse, but by the time they'd arrived, it had been too late. Julie was gone.

The women had held a small private memorial for her, with family and close friends only, and had her ashes buried next to their parents' graves. Samantha and Sarah had stayed the rest of the summer at the house but, at Emily's insistence, both women had reluctantly returned to school in the fall. Sam had trouble getting back into the routine of attending classes and completing assignments, but she'd finally started to hit her stride with a creative memorial she'd written about Julie, and about her life with her sisters, all of which had garnered her much acclaim from one of her favourite professors. As a result, she had slowly managed to buckle down and build on that momentum, eventually giving the finished manuscript to Emily to read as part of her birthday present that year. Emily had loved it to the point of affectionately driving Ryan crazy with her proud boasting of her youngest sister's literary accomplishments.

Ryan had moved into the house by mid-October, just before Sam and Sarah had returned for their first family Thanksgiving dinner without Julie. The atmosphere had remained somewhat somber, despite everyone's best attempts to the opposite, but they all took the trip to the pumpkin farm, including Ryan, and at Samantha's insistence, they altered the family tradition once again.

For the first time, they would have a Jack-o'-Lantern lighting the way for Julie, as well.

When Sam and Sarah returned a few weeks later to carve the pumpkins and light them all for Halloween during and after their annual cemetery visit, the three women, Ryan, and Trick, had all taken a long walk along the river together; both couples strolling hand-in-hand while Trick trotted on ahead, continually stopping to look back and monitor their progress. Together, they'd reminisced quietly on the year which had just passed. Conversation grew sparse for a few minutes, each of them lost in their own private thoughts. Emily broke the silence.

"Can I ask you something?" She turned, looking quizzically at Samantha. Sam nodded slowly.

"Sure," she replied. "I guess so." Emily bit her bottom lip absently as she considered for a moment, then proceeded, choosing her words carefully.

"I was wondering, if it's okay, that is...I was wondering if you'd tell me - tell us - what happened in those last few minutes you had with Jules?" Emily hesitated, blinking back her tears. "I just...I'm not sure I'll ever forgive myself for not being there, you know? In the room with her. After everything. I guess...I just wanted to know if she was...okay..." Her voice trailed off. Samantha took a few slow paces forward, and then stopped, turning to face the others. She lifted her head to gaze into the overhanging branches of the willow tree under which she now stood, and closed her eyes momentarily, a faint smile on her face. Her eyes opened, and fell on each one in turn, finally coming to a rest on Emily.

"Yeah," she answered. "I can tell you now, I think. I'm sorry, I couldn't before...it was like I couldn't even think about it, you know? It hurt too much, thinking about her. I started to just push it all out of my mind. But writing about her - about all of us - that sort of made it easier. And now today...I don't know. It just seems right." Sam took a deep breath in the chilly autumn air. Could it really only have been a year since she'd been last standing by this same river, struggling to keep her guilt, shame and fear hidden from her sisters? So much had happened since then. So much she'd tried to forget. And so much she was slowly learning to embrace. Her last minutes alone with her sister as she'd lay dying being some of the most painful, and most valuable, of them all. She swallowed past the painful lump that had risen in her throat, and continued.

"She was okay," Sam began quietly. "I mean, despite all of the meds she had clouding her over and making her sleepy and delirious most of the time, by then...she was okay. She seemed to be kind of at peace with it all, you know? I think she knew...I think she knew it was her time. And she didn't fight it. She just sort of...went to sleep." Sam blinked back tears of her own before proceeding. "Before she...before...she asked me to do her a favour. I promised I would do whatever it was, whatever I could. So she asked me to - " Sam hitched a sob, and caught her breath painfully in the middle of her chest, suddenly remembering everything so clearly, as though it had all happened just the day before. "'*Carve the light for me, Samie*', she said. She wanted me - wanted us - to carve a pumpkin for her, too. To light her way home, too." Sam's blue eyes filled with tears as she spoke, and Emily reached over to take her hand, tears streaming down her face, as well. Sam ran a flustered hand through her hair, trying to maintain some semblance of control over herself.

"I promised her," Sam wept, as Emily nodded in sympathetic understanding. "I promised her we would...that we all would...always. And then..." Sam shook her head, as if trying to clear it. "Then she mumbled something ... something I couldn't quite catch. She was getting so incoherent by then, and I could only hear parts of it because she was whispering. I had to lean right in close, so I took her hand and tried to hear... It didn't make sense for a second, but then I realized...I knew what she was saying. I should have told you before, I know. I'm sorry, Em. I just couldn't...for a while, I just couldn't...talk..." Sam broke off, and Emily shook her head.

"I understand, Samie, and it's okay. Tell me now, if you can. What else did she say?" Sam's wide, tear-filled blue eyes blinked sadly up at her sister. She could still hear Julie's soft whisper, almost as though she were standing right there next to her, giving voice to the autumn breeze that drifted through the trees, ruffling their hair and tugging tenderly at their jackets. Sam's lips moved, but it was Julie's voice which came through on the gentle wind.

"'*That's where you'll find me*'," she'd whispered. "'*In that one perfect moment, when the world holds its breath, just before the last leaf falls. That's where I'll be..*'"

me ↗   *Not me* ⭐

ABOUT THE AUTHOR

Sue Maynard was born and raised in the rural Canadian village of Creemore, ON (yes, like the beer), but currently hangs her hat in the much bigger metropolis of Mordor...er...Toronto. She is a proud Browncoat, a horror geek girl, and an overall sci fi nerd. In addition to writing, Sue is a total freak for movies, books, video games, comicons, llamas, paperdolls, shiny things, Coke Zero, and her cat.

Carving the Light is Sue's first novel, originally written for the 2009 NaNoWriMo challenge, which marked both her first year as a NaNo participant, and her first recorded 'win'. It also holds the dubious distinction of being the first project of this magnitude that Sue has ever managed to actually complete, as she has not always been the biggest fan of finishing what she starts. Sue has, however, been known to step into a room and immediately map out her escape plan in the case of a zombie attack.

So maybe she's just been conserving her energy for that.

LaVergne, TN USA
03 September 2010
195786LV00003B/93/P